Six winners. Six fantasies.
Six skeletons come out of the closet...

Plain Jane Kurtz is going to use her winnings to discover her inner vixen. But what's it *really* going to cost her?

New girl in town Nicole Reavis is on a journey to find herself. But what *else* will she discover along the way?

Risk taker Eve Best is on the verge of having everything she's ever wanted. But can she take it?

Young, cocky Zach Haas loves his instant popularity, especially with the women. But can he trust it?

Solid, dependable Cole Crawford is ready to shake things up. But how "shook up" is he prepared to handle?

Wild child Liza Skinner has always just wanted to belong. But how far is she willing to go to get it?

Million Dollar Secrets—do you feel lucky?

Blaze™

Dear Reader,

When the concept for this book, *For Lust or Money*, was presented to me, I had some reservations. I'd never attempted an older woman/younger man story. But as I thought about the possibilities, I decided that it might be fun. After all, as a single woman over thirty (and forty, too!), I could relate to the fantasy of falling for a younger man.

Zach Haas isn't just any younger man. He's smart and funny and handsome—oh, and he has millions. How could Kelly Castelle keep from falling in love? Well, it wasn't hard to find reasons.... I simply asked myself what would keep me from falling for a guy eleven years younger than me.

Still, by the end of the book I'd managed to convince myself that it would be possible. Now I just have to find the guy! I hope you enjoy *For Lust or Money*. I certainly enjoyed the challenge of getting these two together for you.

Happy reading,

Kate Hoffmann

KATE HOFFMANN

For Lust
or Money

HARLEQUIN®

TORONTO • NEW YORK • LONDON
AMSTERDAM • PARIS • SYDNEY • HAMBURG
STOCKHOLM • ATHENS • TOKYO • MILAN • MADRID
PRAGUE • WARSAW • BUDAPEST • AUCKLAND

ISBN-13: 978-0-373-79360-0
ISBN-10:   0-373-79360-X

FOR LUST OR MONEY

Printed in U.S.A.

ABOUT THE AUTHOR

Kate Hoffmann lives in a small town in Wisconsin, where she spends her days spinning stories for Harlequin Books. Before penning her first romance novel, published in 1993, Kate was a schoolteacher, an assistant buyer for a department store chain, the head of alumni relations at a university, and an advertising executive. When she isn't writing, she enjoys gardening, golf and genealogy.

Books by Kate Hoffmann

HARLEQUIN BLAZE
234—SINFULLY SWEET
    "Simply Scrumptious"
279—THE MIGHTY QUINNS:
    MARCUS
285—THE MIGHTY QUINNS:
    IAN
291—THE MIGHTY QUINNS:
    DECLAN
340—DOING IRELAND!

**HARLEQUIN
SINGLE TITLES**
(The Quinns)
REUNITED
THE PROMISE
THE LEGACY

HARLEQUIN TEMPTATION
847—THE MIGHTY QUINNS:
    CONOR
851—THE MIGHTY QUINNS:
    DYLAN
855—THE MIGHTY QUINNS:
    BRENDAN
933—THE MIGHTY QUINNS:
    LIAM
937—THE MIGHTY QUINNS:
    BRIAN
941—THE MIGHTY QUINNS:
    SEAN
963—LEGALLY MINE
988—HOT & BOTHERED
1017—WARM & WILLING

1

KELLY CASTELLE was in hell. At least, this was exactly what she imagined hell to be, minus all the traffic and the sidewalks and the buildings. She brushed a wayward strand of hair out of her eyes and dabbed at her damp forehead with her wrist. She'd had her share of awful jobs in the past, but this time, she truly believed she'd find Beelzebub behind the camera.

"Is it always so hot here?"

The driver glanced at her in the rearview mirror. "It's the middle of August, miss," he said. "And it's Atlanta. What did you expect?"

"Something a bit more like L.A.," she muttered. Back home it was warm, but she'd never experienced humidity like this. Her clothes clung to her skin and her hair had gone limp the moment she'd stepped off the plane. *Wilted* would barely do justice to the way she felt. And if she looked even half as bad as she felt, they'd fire her on the spot and hire another actress—one who knew how to look crisp and composed in ninety-five-degree heat.

Maybe this was all just a sign, Kelly mused. Just a week ago, she'd decided that it might be time to get out of Hollywood and show business and find a new life for herself. She'd worked on her acting career, first in New York and then in L.A., for nearly fifteen years and had nothing to show for it. Sure, she'd made a few guest appearances on TV series that had long been cancelled. She'd done some commercials and had a bit part in a cheesy horror movie. She'd even worked on a soap opera for two years before her character got killed off when a meteor fell on her trailer home. But she'd never been able to land a decent agent and she was fast approaching the age when no one would even bother calling her to read.

Thirty-five. There were plenty of actresses who would kill to be her age again. But over the past couple of years, Kelly had heard her career clock ticking down. Women in Hollywood had a short shelf life and she was beginning to mold around the edges.

Just last month, her agent had called to ask if she'd ever considered doing soft-core porn. Kelly would have fired Louise DiMarco on the spot had she not offered a national hemorrhoid commercial in the same breath. She'd turned them both down before Louise made casual mention of a small job in Atlanta, performing in a skit for the talk show *Just Between Us.*

Though it didn't pay much, Kelly didn't care. It was a free trip to Atlanta and a night in a nice hotel and enough money to pay the grocery bill for a few more months. Desperate to get out of L.A., if only for a day or two, she'd jumped at the chance. Though this could hardly be called her big break, at least it wasn't soft-core porn.

But was she fooling herself? A bit part in a six-minute

skit on a talk show could hardly even be compared to a walk-on in a feature film with a third-rate director. She'd have to make some firm decisions about her future once she got back to L.A. For now, she'd just have to focus on doing the best job she could.

"Here we are," the driver said as he pulled up to the curb. "CATL studios. Need help inside with your bag?"

Kelly shook her head and handed him a twenty from her purse. "No, I'm fine. Thanks."

He waved his hand. "The fare is taken care of by the show. The tip, too."

The driver popped the trunk and jumped out of the Town Car, then helped her out of the backseat. Kelly drew a deep breath and stepped out into the heat. She stared at the exterior of the studio, a modern mix of glass and redbrick. Silver letters, spelling out the call sign, gleamed in the noonday sun. She glanced down to see her bag sitting on the curb as the car roared away.

"The show must go on," she muttered.

Dragging her suitcase behind her, Kelly crossed a small courtyard and stepped through the wide glass doors into a cool, quiet lobby. A pretty receptionist sat at a sleek modern desk in front of a glass wall. Sofas and chairs were scattered about in small conversation groups and a bank of television monitors hung from the ceiling behind the receptionist's desk.

Kelly pasted a smile on her face and stepped up to the desk. "Hello, I'm—"

"Miss Castelle," the receptionist completed. She

quickly punched a button on her switchboard. "Hi, Jane. It's Mindy. Miss Castelle is here." The receptionist looked up. "She'll be right out."

"Is there somewhere I could freshen up?"

"Oh, they'll be taking you right back to wardrobe and makeup."

Kelly blinked in surprise. "Makeup?"

"You're scheduled to start shooting at…" Mindy peered at her computer screen. "In a half hour."

"I—I thought we'd have a meeting or a read-through. I didn't think we'd—"

"They work on a really tight schedule back there," Mindy said, a hint of an apology in her tone.

Kelly bent down and frantically searched through her carry-on for her script. She'd glanced at it on the plane, but if she was expected to start taping in thirty minutes, then there was still work to do. She hadn't even thought about her character's goals and motivations. She'd assumed they'd cover that at the read-through.

Oh, hell, what was she worried about? It was skit. A six-minute skit for a local talk show. It would air once and then fade into television obscurity.

"Miss Castelle?"

Kelly struggled to her feet, the script clutched to her chest. "Yes?" The woman standing in front of her was dressed in a funky vintage shirt and black jeans that hugged her slender legs. Her bleached hair was cut in an asymmetrical bob that only makeup artists and wardrobe stylists could pull off.

"I'm Jane Kurtz," she said. "Welcome to Atlanta. I'm

just going to take you back to wardrobe and then we'll get you into makeup." She glanced at her watch. "How was your flight? Hartsfield can be a nightmare but you seemed to have survived it all right."

She held the door open as she let Kelly pass, then led her through a maze of hallways. They came to an open door and Jane stepped inside a large room filled with floor-to-ceiling racks of clothing. "This is Karen Carmichael, my new assistant," Jane said.

Kelly smiled at a dark-haired woman in her late twenties, dressed in a wildly patterned smock. A purple streak colored her ragged bangs and a tiny diamond glittered from one of her nostrils.

"Size two," Karen said. "And five-six?"

Kelly nodded. "Good guess."

Jane grinned. "See, Karen, I knew there was a reason I hired you. Although your ability to guess my weight to the pound is not a talent that I want you to cultivate."

"One hundred and sixteen," Karen said, with another glance at Kelly.

Kelly gasped. "Wow. That's incredible."

Karen looked at Jane. "Couldn't you just kill her? The last time I weighed one-sixteen I was in seventh grade."

Jane chuckled. "I'll kill her after we're done taping."

Kelly glanced between the two of them and saw the humor in their eyes. "You can take some solace in the fact that I'm probably at least five or ten years older than each of you." She paused, then held up three fingers, followed quickly by all five.

"Nicole is going to flip out," Karen said. "You don't look thirty-five. And you're supposed to be the older woman in this skit."

"Don't worry," Jane said. "The guy she's working with looks really young. It'll work. And the lights always add five years."

They continued down the hallway to the makeup room. Jane placed Kelly's bag beneath the counter, then sat her down in a chair in front of a wall of mirrors. A television monitor hung from the ceiling, the sound barely audible.

Kelly stared at her reflection. "My hair looks horrible."

"I've got some miracle hairspray. We'll just tip you upside down and give it a shot and then touch up with a curling iron." Jane ran her fingers through Kelly's hair. "Lovely color," she said. "Who does your color?"

"No one," Kelly replied.

"You do it yourself?"

"No, I don't color my hair. Why, do you think I should color it?"

"No. Don't touch it. I'm just surprised you haven't found any gray yet with your hair as dark as it is."

In truth, Kelly had found more than a few gray hairs at her temples. And she'd been methodically plucking them out, rather than admit that it might be time to visit a good colorist. But now that she wasn't going to be an actress anymore, she wouldn't have to worry. Women had gray hair in the real world. "Not yet," she lied.

As Jane worked, Kelly reviewed the script. *Just Between Us* was an interesting hybrid of all the best elements of talk shows. The host, Eve Best, presented sexy topics, laced with humor and spontaneity, ranging from celebrity gossip to the latest trends in fashion to personal relationships. Lately, the producers had been using skits that resembled reality television, with small scenes interspersed through the show to highlight an upcoming segment. The title on Kelly's script was "In Praise of Younger Men." The smaller segments pointed out the pitfalls and pleasures of an affair with a younger man.

"Hello. You must be the older woman."

Kelly glanced over to find her "younger man" standing in the door. She wasn't sure what she'd expected, but seeing the typical Hollywood "himbo" as her acting partner brought a twinge of disappointment. The guy was gorgeous in that obnoxiously pretty way that was sure to make him look ten times better on screen than she did.

"Hi," she said, forcing a smile. "Kelly Castelle."

"Bryan Lockwood," he countered with a nod and dazzling white smile. "Say, can we move this along? I've got an 8:00 p.m. flight back to the coast and I can't miss it. I'm meeting with Hanks's people tomorrow morning about a part in his new film."

"Tom Hanks?" Kelly asked.

"It's a big part. My agent says I'm perfect for it. And later this week I've got a meeting with Cruise's new production company. The last thing I want is to screw that all up because of this silly job."

"We're almost ready," Jane muttered.

"Cool. I'll see you on set," he said, giving Kelly another dazzling smile.

"What an ass," Jane muttered a few moments after he'd left the room. "That guy was a nightmare in the chair. I had to redo his foundation three times until I got that sunkissed, west-coast, Laguna Beach shade that he wanted." She placed her hands on Kelly's shoulders and met her gaze in the mirror. "I'll let you in on a little secret. He's got a receding hairline. I give him two more years before he's going to need plugs."

"Thanks," Kelly said. "This whole job is really taking a toll on my ego."

"You're gorgeous," Jane assured her. "Look. That classic profile, that perfect nose. Those cheekbones couldn't get any higher." She grabbed a pot of lip liner. "And look at this mouth. All those women who get their lips plumped up have got to be green with envy when they see yours."

"All right, my ego is soothed," Kelly said with a laugh. "No need to overdo."

Jane carefully filled in with lipstick then handed Kelly a tissue to blot. "You're set. Come on, I'll take you out and introduce you to Nicole. She's the segment producer."

Kelly looked at herself in the mirror. She still looked good. There were plenty of actresses her age that looked older. Drawing a deep breath, she cleared her mind of all the insecurities and self-doubts. This was just another acting job. And though it might be the last of her career, she'd be the consummate professional.

And later, when she got back to her hotel, she could

give in to all the emotions that raged inside of her and have a really good cry.

ZACH HAAS STOOD in the shadows of the set, staring through the lens of the television camera at the woman sitting on the park bench. Since she'd walked onto the set, he hadn't been able to take his eyes off of her.

He zoomed in on her face, which was turned in profile, and studied her features. He'd worked behind the camera at *Just Between Us* for six months now and he couldn't recall ever seeing a more extraordinary woman. Every feature of her face was in delicate balance with the others. Perfection, he mused. And just slightly exotic. He couldn't put his finger on her heritage, but it was a tantalizing mix that had given her deep mahogany hair and pale green eyes and smooth porcelain skin.

"All right," Nicole Reavis said, "let's get started. Why don't we do a quick run-through while George adjusts the lighting and then we'll roll tape? We have four short little scenes here. Cultural references, life experiences, sexual compatibility and future happiness. In this first one, you've just met and you're talking about music. Kelly, this is where you realize that Bryan has never really listened to the music that defines your life. And it makes you uneasy." Nicole stepped back and walked back toward the control room. "Whenever you're ready," she called.

They were taping with two cameras and Zach waited to hear Nicole's voice through the headset he wore. She'd give him and John the cues for close-ups and wide shots, as well as calling out directions to the actors over the P.A. system in the studio.

"All right, let's get this on tape," Nicole called after they'd run their lines.

Kelly glanced over at the cameras with a nervous look. "I—I'm used to rehearsing a bit more. Can we just run it a couple more times?"

"Don't worry," Nicole said. "We'll fix any problems in editing. From the top."

Zach focused on Kelly and smiled to himself as she began to deliver her lines. He'd spent a lot of time looking through a camera at all sorts of people and places. Nearly six years in film school, first undergrad in Colorado and then graduate school at City University of New York, had taught him that not everyone looked good on film. But no one had ever looked quite as beautiful as this woman. She was like one of those movie stars from the thirties, glamorous and alluring.

He felt a frisson of desire shoot through him and he drew a ragged breath. Ever since he'd come to Atlanta, he'd been careful to avoid any serious entanglements with the opposite sex. There had been women he'd felt mildly attracted to and women he'd taken to bed. After all, he was twenty-four years old. A guy had needs. But he'd avoided anything that came close to a real relationship.

His needs. That's what had gotten him into trouble in the first place. Or maybe it had been all about the risk, the danger, the kick of seducing an older woman… especially a woman with power. But he'd never expected her to use that power against him. It had cost him every-thing he'd worked for, everything that meant anything to him.

"Zach!"

"I'm here," he murmured to Nicole.

"Pull back a bit."

Zach did as he was told, the murmur of Kelly's voice serving as a soft counterpoint to his thoughts. The day he'd left New York, he'd decided to give up his penchant for older women, but now he had cause to reconsider. Kelly Castelle was the first woman he'd seen in a long time that had caused an immediate and intense reaction. Though she couldn't be that much older than he was. She looked thirty, tops, and what was six years?

"I'm sorry," Kelly said, rubbing her forehead. She looked up. "Can we go back and do that again?"

"If you'd read the line right in the first place, we could all get out of here!"

Kelly gasped, then turned to look at Lockwood. "I just think the pacing is a little quick for this scene."

"Cut!" Nicole shouted.

Zach frowned, then stepped out from behind the camera.

Bryan Lockwood stood up and shook his head, throwing his hands up dramatically. "This is ridiculous. I'm just not feeling it. She's not giving me anything to work with here. What's my motivation? Why would I even take a second look at a woman her age?"

"I'm sorry," Kelly said, her voice trembling slightly.

"I—I'm just used to a bit more rehearsal. Let's do it again. I'm sure I'll be able to get it right—"

"No," Bryan replied, "I'm used to working with professionals. It's obvious you don't know what you're doing."

Zach felt his temper rise. Just who was this jerk? He had no right to talk to Kelly this way. But before he could speak up, Kelly stood up and whacked the guy over the head with her script.

"Listen, you…you little—shit. I was studying acting with some of New York's finest teachers while you were still watching *Barney*. I was doing Shakespeare in the park while you were playing a munchkin in your grade-school production of *The Wizard of Oz*. Don't you dare question my professionalism or my talent. I've been at this for fifteen years. When you've been a working actor for that long, buster, you come and see me and then we'll talk."

"The name's Bryan," he muttered. "Bryan Lockwood. Remember it. You're going to be hearing a lot about me in the next few years."

"The only person who'll remember you in ten years will be your mother."

"I don't need this job," he muttered. "Get yourself some community-theatre castoff to do this." With that, Bryan Lockwood turned on his heel and strode off the set.

"And you better look into hair plugs right now," Kelly shouted after him, "because you're going bald!"

The door slammed behind Lockwood and the studio became eerily silent. Kelly, wide-eyed and flushed with temper, glanced between Nicole and the assistant producer. She swallowed hard, then attempted a smile. "I'm sorry. I—I don't know what got in to me. I've never, ever spoken to a colleague that way." Tears swam in her eyes. "I—I don't know what to say. Please forgive me. I—I'll just be going now."

"Hold it," Nicole said. "You're not going anywhere."

"I—I just assumed you'd be…firing me."

"We'll call in another actor. We'll have to find some-one local. And make a note. We are not paying for Mr. Lockwood's plane ticket home. Geez, what an ass."

"I'm so sorry," Kelly said. "I just don't know what got in to me. I've never done anything like that before, I swear."

Nicole rubbed her temple as if to ease a tension headache coming on. "We're not going to be able to stick to our taping schedule if we have to wait around for another actor."

"I'll do it," Zach said. The words were out of his mouth before he realized he'd said them. He slowly stepped out from behind the camera. "Hey, it doesn't look that hard. And I took some acting classes in college. I'm here and you're paying me anyway, so why don't you let me give it a shot."

He met Kelly's gaze and saw a look of gratitude in her pale green eyes. A tiny smile touched the corners of her sensuous mouth and at that very moment, Zach wondered what it might feel like to kiss her. He'd soon find out since there was a kiss written in to the script.

"I suppose we don't have anything to lose," Nicole said. "Are you sure you want to appear in front of the camera?"

"It'll be an interesting experience," Zach said. "And Larry's been looking for a chance to get behind the camera. He can take my place."

"All right," Nicole said, glancing at her watch. "I'm going to give you two an hour to work this all out and then we'll try taping it. If it doesn't look good, we'll call in another actor for tomorrow." She handed him her script.

A few moments later, they were alone in the studio. Kelly sighed softly. "Thank you. I don't know what to say."

"No problem," Zach said. He was afraid to look at her, afraid that once he did, he'd never be able to drag his gaze away. "So, I guess we should rehearse."

She held out her hand. "I'm Kelly Castelle. Extremely embarrassed actress."

Zach took her fingers into his grasp. The moment he touched her, he felt his blood warm and his pulse quicken. She had such beautiful hands, perfectly tinted nails and long fingers. His mind flashed on an image of her fingers skimming over his chest, then moving lower to his belly, and then lower still. Zach stifled a moan. "Zach," he murmured. "Zach Haas. Accommodating cameraman."

A long silence grew between them. "Maybe we should start?" she said. "We don't have much time."

As they read their lines for the first segment, Zach found himself distracted again and again by a surreptitious study of her face. Even with the cheesy dialogue, she managed to find the true emotion in the script. Her acting seemed so natural and effortless on the surface, but he could sense her analyzing and adjusting as they went along. Obviously the jerk they'd hired to play opposite her hadn't been smart enough to see what she really was. Careful, nuanced…real.

"It's your line."

Zach shook himself out of his distraction. "What?"

"You. It's your line." She paused. "I'm really sorry for this. If you don't want to do this, you don't have to."

"I do," Zach answered. "I do."

She closed her script and smoothed her fingers over the cover. "I don't know what got in to me. I'm usually a very calm person. I can't remember the last time I blew up at someone."

Reaching out, Zach smoothed his palm over the back of her hand. He hadn't thought twice about touching her. It seemed like the most natural thing in the world, to soothe her regrets. "If it's any consolation, he deserved it."

She stared down at his hand, a hesitant smile on her lips. "Still, that's no excuse." Drawing a deep breath, she closed her eyes for a moment. "Maybe I'm having a midlife crisis. Not that I want to run out on my husband and have an affair, but I'm just feeling so restless. Like I need to make a huge change in my life or I'll just go crazy."

"Do you have a husband?" Zach had never considered that prospect. She wasn't wearing a wedding band. But then, she wouldn't wear it if she were playing a single woman in the skit.

"No," Kelly replied.

"Good." He smiled as he traced a long, unbroken line

up her forearm with his fingertip. "I mean, good that you haven't broken any marriage vows. Not good that you're not married. Unless, you don't want to be married. Then it's good."

She giggled and fixed him with a sultry look. "How old are you?"

"Very old," he teased. "Ancient by teenage standards."

"*I'm* old."

"How old?" he asked.

"In Hollywood, everyone is twenty-nine. Besides, it's not polite to ask."

Zach leaned back, stretching his legs out in front of him and linking his hands behind his head. "I don't think age makes any difference."

"The only people who say that are too young to know better," Kelly said.

Zach clutched his chest. "Ouch. That was cruel."

"Age makes all the difference," she said with a serious expression. "At least where I come from."

"You are, without a doubt, one of the most beautiful women I've ever met. And I'd still think that, no matter how many candles you put on your birthday cake."

Kelly blushed. "You may not be old, but you are charming beyond your years."

"How about we just pretend we're the same age?"

"That would be a bit difficult considering the casting of this skit." She glanced down at the script. "We should probably get back to work. We haven't gone over the last segment."

"The bedroom scene? I figured you were saving the best for last."

This time she laughed, a light, musical giggle that echoed through the studio. "You are so cocky."

He grabbed her hand and laced his fingers through hers. "I love it when you talk dirty to me."

"Change of plans!"

Kelly yanked her hand from his and stood up, nervously clutching her script. Nicole swept into the studio and regarded them both with a curious expression. Her eyebrow rose as she gave Zach a disapproving look. "We're going to have to put off taping until tomorrow afternoon. We've got to retape a remote interview for another show before the end of the day. Kelly, we'll have your driver take you back to the hotel. We'll change your plane ticket and get you another night at the hotel. I hope that's all right with you?"

"Fine," Kelly said. "I'll be ready to go tomorrow, I promise."

"Then you've rehearsed everything?" Nicole asked.

"Not everything," Zach quickly said. "But we can get together tonight and run lines. Your hotel?"

His request took her by surprise, but Zach knew she couldn't refuse extra rehearsal, especially in front of Nicole.

"I really think we should keep this on a professional level," she whispered, just out of earshot of Nicole.

"I wasn't suggesting a date," he said, grinning.

"We can meet early tomorrow, before we're scheduled to tape."

Zach wasn't about to give up so easily. He wanted to explore this attraction he had to Kelly and that would take some time outside the studio and away from the prying eyes of his coworkers.

"Zach, can I see you in the hall?" Nicole asked.

He sent Kelly a smile, then followed Nicole. When they reached the hallway, she turned to him.

"Are you sure you took acting classes?" she asked.

Zach nodded. "Three semesters."

"Then you must have missed the lesson where they taught you not to hit on your costars."

Zach chuckled. "I'm just trying to get the best performance I can out of Miss Castelle."

KELLY STARED AT her reflection in the dressing-room mirror. Her face was flushed and her eyes bright and it wasn't until a few minutes ago that she was able to breathe normally.

This was crazy! From the moment Zach Haas had stepped out from behind the camera, she'd been unable to think, unable to do anything more than just lose herself in every detail of his face and his body. The sound of his voice, the color of his eyes, the shape of his mouth. He was one of those incredibly gorgeous young men, the kind who didn't realize the effect they had on women, the kind who made females of all ages weak in the knees.

In the course of a half hour together, she'd managed to convince herself that he was probably the best kisser on the planet, that he had a killer body beneath the baggy cargo pants and T-shirt he wore, and that he could seduce a woman by simply smiling at her.

Yes, he was young. But his playful, boyish nature combined with just a bit of bad-boy attitude and quick-witted intelligence was a lethal combination in a package like that.

She'd pegged his age at twenty-five, give or take two years. If he were only twenty-three, then she was dancing close to perversity. But if he were twenty-seven, then that was nearly thirty. And any man over thirty would be an appropriate choice for her.

Kelly groaned and buried her face in her hands. What was happening to her? Ever since leaving L.A., she felt as if her life were spinning too fast for her to think straight. Was it the heat? Or was she really standing on the precipice of a midlife crisis?

"Are you all right?"

She sat up and looked at Jane's reflection in the mirror, then slowly turned around in the chair. "I'm fine. It's just been a really long day. I got on a plane this morning at 5:00 a.m. and I haven't had a chance to relax since then."

"Your car is waiting out front. He'll drive you back to the hotel and pick you up tomorrow afternoon. We're scheduled to tape at three and Zach will probably be available before then to rehearse. If there's a change, Nicole will call you at the hotel."

"Thanks," Kelly said. She slowly stood. "Again, I'm sorry about all the trouble I caused."

"Don't worry. We're all looking forward to seeing Zach in front of the camera. He's usually the one giving us grief about our jobs, now we can give him some grief about his performance."

"He seems like a really nice guy," Kelly commented, trying to sound objective and uninterested.

"He can be. He's also an incorrigible flirt and too sexy for his own good. Be careful with that one," Jane warned. "I suspect he's talked his fair share of ladies right out of their clothes and into his bed."

"I got that feeling, too," Kelly said, forcing a smile.

"But then, he is legal, so what goes on between consenting adults is…"

"How old is he?" Kelly asked.

"Twenty-four, I think. Maybe twenty-five. He was in graduate film school until he started working for the show last winter."

Twenty-four, Kelly mused. Somehow nine years seemed a whole lot more acceptable than eleven. There was a double-digit difference between them!

"Well," Jane said, "I'll see you tomorrow."

"I'll be here," Kelly replied. She stood up and began to gather her things to change back in to her street clothes. She slowly unbuttoned the silk shirt she wore and let it fall off her shoulders. A soft knock sounded on the door and a moment later it opened. She expected to see Jane again, but Zach stepped inside.

Kelly snatched up the shirt and held it over her chest. "Hi," she said.

Zach's gaze slowly drifted down her body. "Sorry. I didn't mean to—"

Kelly turned her back to him and slipped in to the shirt again, clutching it closed in the front. "What is it?"

"Nothing important," he said.

She faced him, waiting for an explanation. A frown furrowed his brow and he studied her face for a long moment. Then in a few short strides, he closed the distance between them. Before she could even protest, he captured her face between his hands and kissed her, his mouth melting against hers, his tongue delving into the crease of her lips.

When he finally drew back, Kelly couldn't think of anything to say. Should she be angry or insulted? In truth, her mind was whirling. Zach Haas knew exactly how to kiss a woman. He'd obviously had a lot of practice. After all, she'd been fantasizing about it since he'd stepped out from behind the camera and it had been so much better than she could have imagined.

"There. We got that out of the way," he murmured, running a finger along her cheek.

"Out of the way?"

"I knew if we didn't, I'd be thinking about it all night. And since we have to do it in front of the camera tomorrow, I thought we might want to get the…bugs out."

"So that was just practice?" Kelly asked, trying to catch her breath.

"Maybe," he said. "And little bit of curiosity. Should we try again? Practice makes perfect."

She didn't object and he took that as an invitation. He kissed her again, this time lingering over her mouth until she opened beneath him. The kiss was deep and stirring and Kelly felt a delicious warmth course through her body. What harm could it possibly do to kiss Zach Haas? It certainly was one of the more pleasant experiences of her life. And an actress had to prepare for these things. Besides, she needed something to take her mind off the disaster that had made up the day's events. Now, at least she had a bright spot to look back on.

"Maybe we should rehearse tonight," Kelly suggested.

A wide grin broke over Zach's face. "I think that would be a very good idea. I want to make sure we get it right. It needs to be believable." He slowly backed toward the door, keeping his eyes fixed on her face. "I'll call you when I get done at the station."

"Yes, call me," she said. "I'm staying at the Sheraton."

"I know," he murmured. "Everyone from the show stays there. I'll see you later, then."

"See you," Kelly said, giving him a little wave.

When the door closed behind him, she drew a deep breath and groaned. Oh, God, what was she doing? Every instinct told her to keep her relationship with Zach strictly professional. And every impulse told her to do the opposite. He was just so…hot! And it had been a long time since she'd indulged in the pleasures that a man's body offered.

There had been boyfriends over the years, but Hollywood romances were always rather shallow and short-lived. And Kelly had a unique talent for picking men who were emotionally unavailable. Whenever things came close to getting serious, they usually headed for the door.

She once visited a therapist to try to sort it all out and the woman had claimed it was Kelly who was deliberately choosing men who wouldn't stay because *she* was the one afraid of commitment, afraid of anything coming between her and her career. But who cared about commitment? All she wanted was a chance to kiss Zach Haas again.

Kelly reached up and touched her lips, still damp from his tongue. Her heart was still pounding at a rapid rate and she could barely draw a breath without growing dizzy. She felt silly and nervous and overwhelmed. What difference did age really make anyway? Hell, any man who kissed as well as he did was no novice to seduction. They were two consenting adults who were attracted to each other, so there was nothing standing in the way.

She was just a little bit more adult than he was.

2

KELLY RELAXED in the backseat of the Town Car as it sat stalled in rush-hour traffic. She pulled out her day planner and wrote down her call time for the next day, then flipped through the pages, searching for the number of her yoga instructor. She traded acting lessons for private yoga instruction and she'd made plans to meet with Katie tomorrow morning. Plans that would have to be cancelled. "McCready," she murmured.

As she was looking through her planner, she passed a familiar name. Angie McMahon. Sweet Nothings. Atlanta, Georgia. She and Angie had been roommates—and best friends—seven years ago, until Angie gave up acting to marry a businessman from Atlanta. They hadn't spoken in almost two years, but still exchanged long letters with each Christmas and birthday card they sent.

"Are we near Buckhead?" Kelly asked the driver.

"About five minutes away," he said. "But your hotel isn't in Buckhead."

"I'm not going to the hotel. I want to go somewhere else if that's all right."

"Wherever you want to go, miss," he said. "You just

have to be there by six. I've got to make a run out to the airport for a pickup."

"I can grab a cab back to the hotel," she said. "The shop is called Sweet Nothings." Kelly read off the address and the driver nodded, then made a lane change when they reached the next intersection and turned right. Within minutes, they were moving more quickly.

She and Angie had shared a tiny two-bedroom apartment in West Hollywood for almost three years, while they were both trying to break in to television work. One night, they'd gone out clubbing and Angie had met Joe Sheppard, a devastatingly charming thirty-five-year-old in town on business. After a long-distance romance, they'd fallen in love and married in a lavish ceremony in Santa Barbara. Now, Angie had a four-year-old daughter and owned a lingerie store.

The driver found the location in a matter of minutes and dropped her and her overnight bag at the curb. Kelly walked up to the door and saw by the sign that the shop was open until six on Tuesday evenings. How would it be to see Angie again? They barely had anything in common anymore, beyond the friendship they'd once shared. And at times, Kelly had envied Angie's happy marriage and her new family. Her friend had given up her dreams of stardom and simply exchanged them for a better dream.

Kelly opened the door, then set her bag just inside and strode up to the counter. "I think my boyfriend is stealing my underwear," she said in desperate tone, recalling an old joke between them. "And he likes to wear it. Do you think we should break up?"

Angie glanced up and a wide smile broke across her face. "Kelly Castelle! What are you doing here?" She hurried around the end of the counter and threw her arms around Kelly's neck, hugging her tight. "I can't believe it's you. Gosh, look at you. You haven't changed a bit."

"I'm here for a job. I'm doing a segment for *Just Between Us*."

Angie stepped back. "The talk show? Really? How long are you going to stay?"

"Tonight and tomorrow night."

"Oh, that's so great! We can have dinner tonight. Joe is out of town on business and Caroline is at Joe's sister's place for a birthday sleepover. I'm a single woman. At least for one night."

Kelly thought about the offer for a long moment. She didn't really have firm plans with Zach, just plans to make plans. And she had enough trouble controlling herself in his presence. It wouldn't do to tempt the attraction she felt toward him with an evening of kissing rehearsal. "All right. We'll have dinner."

"Oh, drinks first and then dinner. God, I can't believe you're here. It seems like ages ago that we lived together. I miss having a roommate. It's so hard to talk to Joe about that time in my life. He just doesn't get it."

"It does seem like it was ages ago." Back then, they were both twenty-seven or twenty-eight and still full of hope about their future. They'd tell each other nearly every day that their big breaks were just around the corner.

"You haven't changed," Angie said. "I think you might have even gotten more beautiful. I've been watching for you on television and checking your page on IMD."

"My career has slowed down a little. Ever since I got written off on the soap, I've just had a few jobs. Nothing big." Kelly took a deep breath. "In fact, I'm thinking about getting out of acting. I'm going to look for a real job—a normal job. Maybe sell real estate or get a job in casting."

"Oh, you should move here!" Angie said, her eyes full of excitement. "I need someone to help manage the store. I'm opening up another location in midtown and I can't be two places at once. And you'd love Atlanta. It's got everything that L.A. has, except people are real here. And everything doesn't revolve around the movies. And you don't have to even think of plastic surgery until you're at least forty."

Kelly shook her head. "I don't know. I haven't really decided where I'll settle. Just that I have to make a change."

Angie glanced at her watch. "Come on, let's get out of here. It's nearly six. I'm the boss and if I want to close early, I can!"

She grabbed her purse from beneath the counter, locked the register and then slipped her arm through Kelly's. "My car is parked out back. Where should we go?"

They ended up at the bar at the Sheraton. Kelly checked in, then made a quick trip up to her room to wash her face and change. By the time she got back downstairs, Angie had already ordered them a pair of cosmopolitans and was chatting up the handsome bartender.

After three drinks and a lot of memories, it seemed as if only a few hours had passed, instead of seven years. Kelly hadn't had a roommate since Angie had left and she realized she hadn't had a best friend, either. She needed someone to confide in, someone who'd understand all the changes she was going through, someone to help sort through the confusion.

"So, tell me about your sex life," Angie said, getting right to the point.

"I don't have one."

"Oh, come on. All those gorgeous men in L.A. and you aren't dating someone?"

"For every gorgeous man there are three gorgeous women. And two of them are younger than me." Kelly gnawed on her lower lip. "Actually, there is someone I'm interested in. The only problem is that he's younger."

"Younger is good," Angie said. "Like a few years younger? Or boy-toy younger?"

"Eleven years," she replied.

Angie's eyes went wide. "Oh, my. That's definitely boy-toy." She took another sip of her drink. "Is he wonderful in bed? Please tell me all the details. I've been sleeping with the same man for seven years and I'd like to imagine someone out there is having wild and crazy sex. Not that we don't have our moments. My talents as an actress have come in handy on more than one occasion, though I've been typecast as the French maid."

"We haven't done anything yet," Kelly admitted. "In truth, I just met him today. There was just a…a spark. I know he's interested and the more I think about it, the more I think I might be interested, too. Or maybe *curious* is a better word. And I think I'm reading the signals right, though I can't be absolutely sure."

"I don't think the signals have changed over the years," Angie said. "Why not go for it?"

Kelly groaned. "Because he's twenty-four, for starters. Isn't that reason enough?"

"No. Men at that age are in their sexual prime, they're adventurous and uninhibited and…energetic. They say that older women should be with younger men because they're a better match in bed, orgasmically that is."

Her answer did make sense and Kelly was forced to rethink her position. Maybe it was that simple. Maybe, when it came to sex, younger was better. "God, he's so gorgeous," Kelly said. "And he's not an actor, so I don't have to worry about him spending the entire evening talking about himself. He's just a regular guy with a beautiful face and killer body and this bad-boy smile that just makes me want to tear off all my clothes and give him everything he wants."

"Then why the indecision?"

"It would just be sex," Kelly said, wincing. "There's no future with him. I thought I gave that kind of thing up a long time ago. I'm older and I'm supposed to be wiser and less self-indulgent."

"You're older, but you also have the maturity to take pleasure where it's offered," Angie said. She picked up her drink. "Here's to new experiences. And new beginnings. Maybe you've found more than you expected here in Atlanta." She downed the rest of her drink then set the glass on the table. "It's time for me to go home. I'm a little drunk and I'm horny and I'm going to call my husband and force him to have phone sex with me."

"You can't drive."

"I'll take a cab and come back and get my car in the morning. The shop doesn't open until ten. If I'm up early, maybe we can have breakfast. We can talk a little more about that job I have for you."

They walked out to the lobby together and Kelly gave Angie a hug. "It's been so nice to see you again. And let's definitely have breakfast tomorrow. I don't want to leave without seeing you again."

"Call me," Angie murmured. "Or I'll call you. Better yet, I'll just stop by."

Kelly watched as she walked out of the lobby, giving her a little wave. The bellman motioned for a cab and a moment later, Angie slipped in to the backseat. Kelly smiled as she walked over to the elevators. It was only eight, but she felt as if she'd been awake for days. She hadn't eaten, so she'd order something light from room service then crawl into bed and sleep.

She closed her eyes as the elevator climbed to the twelfth floor. She could sleep or she could call Zach Haas and invite him over. No doubt there'd be a message from him waiting on her voice mail. Kelly giggled softly. God, was she really considering making a booty call?

The elevator doors opened and she walked down the hall

toward her room, weighing her options. Kelly noticed a man sitting on the floor near her room door, his attention focused on his cell phone. She hesitated for a moment, then recognized Zach. "Oh, boy. Here we go," she murmured to herself.

With every step she took, she felt as if she were walking in to dangerous territory. The sexual attraction between them was undeniable and incredibly intense. And a man like Zach was probably used to acting on his urges and getting exactly what he wanted whenever he wanted it. She'd lived her life within the lines for so long. Was she really ready to step out and do something so bold and daring?

He stood up as she approached, tucking the phone in his jacket pocket as he leaned back against the wall. Kelly reached in to her purse and withdrew her key card. He watched her the whole time and she tried to keep her hands from trembling.

"I was about to leave," he murmured.

She sent him a sideways glance, their gazes meeting for a long moment. Kelly felt a shiver run down her spine at the look in his eyes—confident, determined, a bit predatory. He had one thing on his mind and she knew what would happen if she let him into her room. He'd find a way to seduce her and she wouldn't be able to stop him. "I'm surprised you came," she said.

"I was in the neighborhood."

"How did you know my room number?"

"The production crew is in and out of this hotel all the

time. Since we pay for the rooms, the front desk gives us the numbers."

Kelly slid the card into the lock and the door clicked. She pushed it open, then turned back to him. "Can you just wait out here for a second?"

"Sure," he murmured.

She slipped inside the room and closed the door behind her, then hurried to the bathroom. The fluorescent light over the sink flickered on and Kelly stared at herself in the mirror. Running her fingers through her hair, she tried to calm herself. "Nothing will happen if you don't want it to," she said to herself.

But the truth was, she did want something happen. She wanted to cast aside everything she'd always known about sex and start again. Only this time, she'd find the spontaneity in it, the all-consuming passion that had always been lacking in her relationships with men. She could be a different woman with this man, could test the boundaries of her need. It would be so simple, one night together with no strings and no expectations—and absolutely no inhibitions.

So what was holding her back? "Fear," Kelly said. What if it was so wonderful that the memory stayed with her for the rest of her life? What if every man she met in the future were measured by one night spent with a twenty-four-year-old stranger?

Or what if she didn't measure up? What if he found her too repressed or too nervous...or too old? Though she kept in good shape, her body wasn't perfect. He was probably used to a twenty-year-old butt and fake boobs and skin that was smooth and tanned and tight. She'd fought her battles with cellulite and she'd lost.

"Oh, God," Kelly said. She unbuttoned her blouse and looked down at her chest. Maybe she should have gotten the boob job when she'd had the cash. She was so completely unprepared for this. She should be wearing black underwear, not this silly leopard print. And she should have fixed her hair and taken time with her makeup and put on a bit of perfume. Oh, and then there were condoms. She didn't have condoms!

A knock sounded on the door and Kelly quickly buttoned her blouse and hurried back into the room. She pulled the door open and peered out.

"If you're going to be much longer, can you get me a beer from the minibar?" Zach asked. "And some peanuts if they have them."

Kelly opened the door. "Sorry. I just needed a moment."

Zach strolled inside. "Let me guess, you had to put on your nice underwear?"

"Very funny. I always wear nice underwear."

He walked over the minibar and pulled out a beer. "Can I make you a drink?"

"No. I've had enough to drink for one night." Her face felt flushed and she blamed it on the cosmopolitans she had shared with Angie, not on her nerves. She'd been with plenty of men. This was just one more. He had all the same equipment, all the same body parts. She'd studied the operator's manual and knew what to do with him. So why was she so nervous?

"It might help you relax," Zach said.

"Do I seem tense? I'm not. Not at all." Kelly grabbed her purse. "If you'll excuse me, I have to run down to the lobby. I need to buy some toothpaste before the gift shop closes. I'll be right back."

She hurried to the door and slipped out into the hallway. This was horrible. She was a wreck and he was probably regretting his decision to see her outside of the studio. If she intended to have one night of incredible sex, then she needed to pull herself together and at least appear as if she were interested—and capable. She rode the elevator back down to the lobby and headed toward the gift shop. Of course they'd have condoms. People had sex all the time in hotels.

She wandered through the small store, past the T-shirts and the coffee mugs, the magazine rack and the stuffed animals, to the corner that featured the toiletries. She found the condoms in boxes of three. They came in a variety of brands...and sizes. The last time she'd shopped for condoms, there was only one size.

Kelly grabbed a box of regular and a box of XLs, then walked to the checkout stand. A young man stood behind the counter. He smiled at her as she set her purchases down. Then he rang them both up. That's twenty-four ninety-three," he said.

"What?"

"That will be twenty-four ninety-three," he repeated.

"For six condoms? Good grief, when did sex get so expensive?"

The young man leaned forward. "If you go on over to the CVS, they're a much better buy. We kind of count on the fact that folks need 'em in a hurry and they're willing to pay."

Kelly reached in to her purse and pulled out her wallet, but she'd spent the last of her cash on drinks with Angie. "Can you put these on my room bill?" she asked.

"Sure, what room?"

Kelly opened her mouth to tell him, then realized that the show was paying for the room. They wouldn't be too thrilled to see condoms on the bill. "Tell me something," she whispered. "If I put these on my bill, will they be itemized?"

The young man shook his head. "No," he whispered back. "It will just say *gift shop*. For all anyone knows, you bought twenty-four ninety-three worth of potato chips and candy bars."

Kelly tucked the condoms into her purse and signed the tab. "Thanks. You've been very helpful." She walked out of the store and back to the elevator.

"Have fun!" the clerk called, his voice echoing into the hallway.

"That's exactly what I intend to do," Kelly muttered.

ZACH GRABBED THE REMOTE from the bedside table and flipped on the TV, running through the channels until he found ESPN. He slid a pillow behind his back and kicked off his shoes, stretching out his legs in front of him. This was the strangest date he'd ever had, if it could even be called a date.

After the kiss they'd shared that afternoon, Zach had looked forward to spending some time with her, knowing where that one kiss would inevitably lead. He couldn't recall ever being so focused on seducing a woman as he was on seducing Kelly Castelle. And he'd thought she was equally interested in him.

But now he wasn't sure where he stood with her. Kelly seemed almost afraid to be in the same room with him. Was she having second thoughts? If so, what was the hangup?

Maybe she *was* married. Maybe she did have a husband waiting for her back in L.A. And maybe she was contemplating cheating. Zach tipped his head back and ran his fingers through his hair. This was becoming a problem with him—he jumped in to sexual relationships with complicated women, seducing them before he even had a chance to examine the luggage they brought to bed with them.

He took a long sip of his beer, then dumped a handful of peanuts into his palm. Maybe it was the age thing, he mused. Women could be really strange about that. He'd always found older women attractive. They were smarter, more sure of themselves, much more fun in bed. And more exciting than the cookie-cutter girls in their early twenties that populated the clubs in Atlanta.

Zach glanced at the door. He climbed off the bed, beer in hand, and wandered into the bathroom. Kelly's things were spread out over the marble vanity. He reached out and picked up a bottle of perfume and held it to his nose. The scent was familiar, causing a current of desire to race through him. He picked through her makeup, looking at lipsticks and eye shadows, then held up a pink razor and ran it over his cheek.

A pretty flowered bag sat next to the sink and he peered inside, only to see a tube of toothpaste and a small bottle of mouthwash.

He shook his head and walked back out into the bedroom. The toothpaste was obviously an excuse to get out of the room. A few moments later, he heard the key in the lock and hopped back onto the bed, stretching his feet out in front of him again. Kelly slipped back inside, her purse clutched in her hand.

She started toward the bed, then stopped. "I'm just going to go brush my teeth. I'll be right back."

He heard her talking to herself in the bathroom and Zach quietly crossed the room to listen at the door. But then the door flew open and he jumped back. "I'm sorry," he said. "I couldn't hear you. Were you talking to me?"

"I—I was talking to myself." Kelly cleared her throat. She ran her fingers through her hair, then walked into the room and stood at the end of the bed. "I think I will have that drink now."

He settled himself back on the bed as he watched her walk to the minibar, his gaze taking in her slender body. She was graceful as she moved, like a dancer, with delicate limbs and perfect posture. He imagined what it might be like to hold that body against his, to slowly remove each piece of her clothing until she was completely naked.

Kelly busied herself mixing a small bottle of vodka

with a can of cranberry juice. "I'm sorry I wasn't here when you got here," she said. "I didn't think you'd come without calling."

"I was just in the neighborhood."

She sent him a sideways glance, then took a long swallow of her drink. "I went out with a friend. A girl-friend. She lives here in Atlanta." She sat down on the end of the bed, her back to him.

For a long time, neither one of them spoke. He took a sip of his beer. For Zach, seduction had always been a fairly straightforward process, but with Kelly he felt as if he had to tread a bit more carefully. She gave new meaning to the word *skittish*.

"Did you bring your script?" she asked.

"No," Zach said. Perhaps she needed the pretense of re-hearsal to make her more comfortable. "We can use yours." He slid down to sit beside her and she immediately stood up.

"Right. Really, we should be off script by this point."

"Are you nervous?" he asked, his gaze dropping to her fingers, which were tightly twisted together. "You seem tense."

"No," she murmured, then paused. "Yes. A little bit."

"We're not going to do anything here that you don't want to do," Zach said, leaning back to rest on his elbows.

Her gaze flitted over his body, stopping briefly at his crotch. "What do you want to do?" she asked, her green eyes wide.

He reached out and grabbed her hand, weaving his fin-gers through hers. "I want to do it all."

She swallowed hard. "I've never done anything like this before," she said, her voice cracking slightly.

This was not going well at all, Zach mused. The attraction between them was electric, crackling between them, but Kelly was so cautious that stealing a kiss might be too much for her to handle. He decided to backtrack a bit. "But you rehearse all the time."

"Is—is that what we're doing?" she asked.

"What did you think we'd be doing?" Keeping her off balance was the best approach, he decided. When they finally gave in to their desire, he wanted her desperate and determined. He wanted the fiery, passionate woman he'd seen through the camera lens, the woman he'd been obsessing about the entire afternoon.

"I'm worried about the bedroom scene," Zach continued. "I was hoping you could give me some tips. We're supposed to kiss and I'm not sure how that's going to happen. Do we figure out ahead of time who goes which way? Or do we just let it happen, as if we're doing it for real?"

"We already did it for real," she said, staring at him with a suspicious glint in her eye. "In my dressing room."

"And that was good? I mean, for a screen kiss?"

A tiny smile curled the corners of her mouth. "Yes, that was very good. I think if we just do it like that, we'll be fine."

"Good to know," he answered, nodding his head. He took another sip of his beer and pointed to the television. "Good game. The Padres are at the top of their division. They've got a really good pitcher from—"

"Maybe we should try it again," Kelly interrupted. "Just to be sure we have it right."

"All right. We should probably lie on the bed. That's what the script says. And as long as we have a bed here, we should put it to use." He shimmied back until he was lying with his back resting against the pillows. "All right," Zach said. "Now, you would be right here." He patted the spot beside him, then set his beer down on the bedside table.

She left her drink on the dresser and sat down on the opposite edge of the bed, folding her hands on her lap. "Shouldn't you be lying down, too?" he asked.

Kelly kicked her feet up on the bed.

"So, you want me to start?"

He moved closer and her gaze fixed on his mouth. She licked her lips and he did the same. "Sure," she said softly. She waited, holding her breath as he slowly leaned forward. But at the last minute, he turned his head the opposite way and their noses bumped.

"Sorry," Zach said. "I thought you were going the other way."

"No, once you start moving toward me, I'll just stay the way I am."

"Right," he said. "Okay. Let's give this another try." He moved in and at the last minute, feinted to the left. She took his cue and tipped her head in the opposite direction and, this time, Zach deliberately missed her mouth completely, kissing her chin instead.

"This shouldn't be so difficult," she said, her voice tinged with frustration. "We've already done it before."

"That time it was more spontaneous," Zach explained. "I wasn't concentrating so hard."

"Well, stop thinking then," she said. "Just do it." She sighed deeply. "Like this." Kelly cupped his face in her hands and pressed her mouth to his. Gradually, the kiss softened as his tongue teased at her lips. She opened her mouth and he lost himself in her sweet taste. It had taken them a while to get here, but it was worth the wait, he mused.

Zach slipped his arms around her waist and pulled her onto the bed to lie on top of him. A tiny moan slipped from her lips as he furrowed his fingers through her silken hair and molded her mouth to his. He couldn't recall ever needing to kiss a woman as much as he needed to kiss Kelly. It was like a hunger inside him that ached to be satisfied. But the more he tasted, the hungrier he became—Kelly was like the Chinese food of kissing.

The buildup, the anticipation, had been almost too much to bear and he was already aroused, his erection pressing against her belly. There was no time to think about consequences or regrets, about mistakes he'd made in the past. This was about lust, pure and simple—the need for two people to take pleasure in each other.

His hands skimmed over her body, her shoulders and then her arms, her torso and her hips. She twisted above him, her fingers clutching at his T-shirt. Zach slipped his hands beneath her blouse and ran his palms up and down her back, every shift of her body causing a wave of pleasure to race through him.

Her skin felt incredible, like warm silk, soft against his hands. Zach forgot everything that had come before, all the hesitation and indecision, and gave himself over to pure sensation. The scent of her hair, the taste of her mouth, the sounds of their breathing mingling together, quick and shallow and desperate.

Any indecision she'd felt earlier was gone and Kelly was now an equal partner in this seduction. When he kissed her, she kissed him back. When he touched her, her hands found a new spot on his body.

Zach drew her leg up along his thigh. His palm skimmed along her rib cage, then over her flat stomach as he stared down into her eyes. "This isn't rehearsal anymore, is it?"

Kelly drew in a quick breath, surprised by his comment. "Did you want to rehearse?"

"No," Zach replied. He furrowed his hands through her silky hair and pulled her closer. "I think this is a much better use of our time, don't you?"

KELLY SLOWLY OPENED her eyes. Light spilled into the room through the sheer drapes and she squinted against the morning sun. A tiny headache nagged at the spot between her eyes and she reached up to rub at the pain. It was only then that she felt the body beside her.

Holding her breath, she turned to look into Zach's face. He was lying on her pillow, his dark hair mussed and his lips slightly parted. He'd discarded his shirt and the top button of his cargo pants was undone. And his feet were bare.

Kelly closed her eyes and let her mind drift back to the events of the previous evening. She'd prepared herself for a night of wild sex and a morning of guilty regrets. But to her surprise, they'd gone no further than kissing and caressing. She was left with no regrets, just a warm, satisfied feeling inside.

To her surprise, Zach had been a gentleman, waiting for her cues to move forward. And though she had been curious, kissing Zach had been an adventure in itself. He elevated the activity to an art. He could be sweet and soft and then turn fierce and demanding. Every need, every emotion he felt, was conveyed through his lips and tongue. And to be honest, Kelly had to admit that kissing him had been more exciting than anything else she'd ever experienced with a man.

She looked at him again, taking in the tiny details of his face, the scar on his forehead, the mole near his left eye, the way the corners of his mouth curled up, even while he was sleeping. With youth came the ability to look good in the morning, and he looked irresistible.

But Kelly knew she wasn't quite as blessed. She carefully crawled out of bed, taking care not to wake him, and walked to the bathroom. The sight that greeted her was enough to make her groan. Her hair looked like a flock of birds might set up housekeeping at any moment. And her makeup was smudged beneath her eyes. And a big red crease ran down her cheek from a fold in the pillowcase.

She quickly stripped out of her clothes and tossed them aside, then turned on the shower. If they were going to continue where they'd left off, she'd need to look a bit more alluring.

She stepped beneath the warm flood of water and closed her eyes. It felt wonderful to finally wash away the stickiness of August in Atlanta. She rinsed her hair, then grabbed the tiny bottle of shampoo that the hotel provided. As she worked the lather through her hair, an unbidden fantasy crept in to her thoughts.

She imagined Zach waking up in an empty bed. He'd look around, wonder where she was, and then he'd hear the shower. He'd walk to the bathroom and slip through the door, then stand silently on the other side of the curtain. Then slowly, he'd strip off his clothes and pull the curtain back. And then, she'd step into his arms and their naked bodies would touch for the very first time.

Kelly drew a ragged breath. Oh, it was a wonderful fantasy, like an erotic movie running in her head. But the most wonderful thing about it was that it could actually happen. She stood beneath the water for a long time as she ran her soapy hands over her skin. But when her fingers began to get pruny, Kelly gave up on the fantasy and shut off the water. She grabbed a towel and dried her hair, then wrapped another around her body.

She opened the door and peered out, but Zach hadn't stirred. He was still sound asleep, his head on her pillow. Kelly grabbed her comb and slowly began to pull it through the tangles in her hair. But as she did, she heard a knock on the door.

Holding the towel at her chest, she walked to the door

and looked through the peephole. Angie was standing on the other side. She opened the door.

"Good, you're up!" Angie cried. "Get dressed. I'm taking you to breakfast. We have to find one of those all-you-can-eat buffets because I want pancakes and sausage and—"

Kelly pressed a finger to her lips. "Shhh!"

"Don't worry. I'm awake."

She spun around to see Zach standing at the end of the bed, his cargo pants hanging low on his hips, his eyes sleepy. He smiled and gave Angie a little wave. "Hi, there," he murmured. "I'm Zach."

Angie giggled softly. "The younger man?" she murmured beneath her breath.

"Yes," Kelly whispered.

"The younger man who spent the night in your room?"

"Yes."

"You know, I can hear everything you're saying," Zach commented. "Us younger guys have really good hearing. And I can see right through that towel. We have X-ray vision, too."

Angie stepped past Kelly, into the room, her hand extended. "Hi. I'm one of Kelly's oldest friends, Angie Sheppard. Actually, Angie McMahon Sheppard."

He took her hand. "Zach Haas. It's nice to meet you, Angie."

"Oh, it's a pleasure to meet you, Zach. I understand you work for *Just Between Us*. I just love that Eve Best. She is so funny and smart. And sassy. Is she that way in real life?"

Kelly felt a blush warm her cheeks and she gently took Angie's arm and pulled her toward the door. "Can you wait for me downstairs? I'll be down in just a minute."

"Take all the time you want," Angie whispered. She gave Kelly a silly expression then mouthed the word *gorgeous*. "I'll meet you in the restaurant. I'm pretty sure I saw a breakfast buffet when I walked past."

Kelly slowly closed the door and turned back to Zach. He was grinning, finding great amusement in her situation. "So you talked with your friend about me?"

"I just mentioned we'd met."

He nodded. "I see." He slowly approached her and Kelly backed up until she stood against the door. Zach placed his hands on either side of her head and bent down to kiss her. His lips were soft, the kiss fleeting. "Morning," he murmured.

Kelly felt her knees go weak and her head begin to spin. "Morning," she said. She clutched the towel tightly at her chest and wondered what might happen if she'd simply let go. *Let go,* her mind repeated over and over again. Why not just…

She loosened her fingers and the towel dropped silently to the floor. Zach's breath caught in his throat and he drew back to look into her eyes. She stared up at him, unflinchingly, daring him to take what she offered, yet afraid that he might not.

His hand slowly moved to her shoulder, smoothing over the length of her neck before dropping lower to cup her breast. Kelly closed her eyes as he gently caressed her nipple with his thumb. She wasn't nervous at all now. This seemed so perfectly right, a fantasy come to life.

A moment later, his lips closed over the taut peak and she furrowed her hands through his hair and moaned softly. And then he dropped to his knees in front of her, his tongue trailing across her belly.

Everywhere he kissed, he left a damp imprint, a reminder that he'd tasted that part of her body and moved on. His hands smoothed over her backside, drawing her closer, and when he kissed her inner thigh, Kelly felt a shiver of desire wash across her skin.

She knew what he wanted and she anticipated how it would feel. But when his tongue found the soft folds of her sex, a shudder of pleasure wracked her body. She gasped, her eyes flying open with the shock of sensation.

Bracing her hands behind her on the door, Kelly arched into him as his tongue flicked at her clitoris. She'd never felt anything quite so wonderful, so achingly powerful. He controlled her with his mouth, meting out pleasure a tiny bit at a time until she was frantic for release.

She didn't want to give in. Instead, she wanted the desire to last forever, to be caught in this whirlwind of pleasure, this precarious balance between hunger and release. Her body belonged to him now, completely and irrevocably, and she wanted to surrender completely.

He knew exactly what he was doing to her and he seemed to take delight in teasing her. Kelly groaned and grasped his hair, gently tugging him even closer. Her body felt boneless, as if any moment it might melt. She wanted him inside her, but she was afraid to want more, afraid that this desire would consume her completely. This was already too much.

She felt the ache building inside her and suddenly, she couldn't fight it any longer. She wanted to let go, to give Zach what he sought. She held her breath and let the pleasure build and then, as if the floodgates burst, she felt the orgasm wash over her. Her body jerked, then dissolved into delicious spasms.

The power of it all took her breath away, made her dizzy. Her fingers tangled in his hair as she pulled his head back, suddenly too sensitive for his caress. When the last spasm subsided, Zach pressed his damp mouth to her belly, nuzzling against her.

"Oh, my," she breathed.

He got to his feet and cupped her face in his hands, then touched his lips softly to hers. "I have to go," he murmured. "I was due at the studio a half hour ago. But I'll see you this afternoon. And tonight, we'll pick up where we left off."

"All right," Kelly repeated, breathlessly.

Chuckling softly, he bent to pick up her towel and wrapped it back around her body. Then he led her to the bathroom. "Are you gonna be all right?"

"I'm fine," Kelly said.

He nodded, then disappeared. A minute later, he was back at the door, only to find her standing in the same spot, the towel clutched in her hand. She couldn't seem to move, even though she knew she ought to.

"Angie's waiting downstairs in the restaurant. You'd better get moving." He stepped into the bathroom and gave her another quick kiss, then pointed at the mirror. "Dry your hair and then get dressed."

"Right," Kelly said.

She heard the room door close behind him and she sank down to sit on the edge of the tub. Pressing her hand to her chest, she forced herself to breathe normally. What was happening to her? Was it the heat? Or had she caught some kind of travel-induced dementia?

She'd never in her life felt anything like this…so intense, so shattering. Whenever she came within three feet of Zach Haas, she found herself compelled to test the limits of her inhibition and she'd found herself stunned by her reaction to his touch. How could she be expected to resist him? He was like a fantasy come to life—a young, virile guy who could make her feel as if there were no end to her desire for him.

She had one more night in Atlanta. The old Kelly Castelle might have spent the evening alone, locked in her hotel room, watching public television and reading the *Tourist's Guide to Atlanta.* But the new Kelly was determined to entice Zach back into her bed and, this time, enjoy every pleasure that his flesh offered.

But before that, she'd go to the studio and pretend she was in love with a younger man. She wondered if the cameras would see that it wasn't such a far-fetched idea. Falling in love with Zach Haas would be as easy as falling off a log. But she couldn't afford to do that, so she would settle for simple lust. For Kelly, that would have to be enough.

3

ZACH STOOD IN FRONT of the dressing-room mirror in a pair of plaid boxers. Now he knew exactly how male actors felt in this situation—like a piece of meat. Suddenly, the body he'd grown quite comfortable with seemed to be full of flaws. His arms weren't big enough and his chest wasn't very cut. And he had four-pack, instead of six-pack, abs. And he'd never even considered waxing the line of hair that ran from the center of his chest to beneath the waistband of his boxers.

"I don't know about the boxers," Karen said, glancing over at Jane. "I think younger guys are probably more in to boxer briefs, don't you?"

"I don't want the audience focused on his butt," Nicole murmured, her brow furrowed into a frown. "And if we put him in boxer briefs I think it's going to be all about the butt."

"I can see your point," Jane commented.

"Can I say something here?" Zach asked.

"No!" All three of them spoke at the same time and Zach got the distinct impression they were enjoying this.

"We could try him in tighty whities," Karen suggested.

"No way." Zach held up his hands. "I haven't worn those since I was ten."

"What do you wear?" Jane asked.

"I think that's a bit personal," Zach said.

"Hey, we're just asking a young guy like yourself what kind of underwear other young guys wear."

"Guys my age like the boxer briefs," Zach said. "But personally, I go commando."

Eve Best poked her head in the open door of the dressing room. "There will be no going commando on my set. I like the boxers. Maybe go with something a little more playful than plaid, though."

"The boss has spoken," Nicole said with a smile. She handed Zach a pair with alligators printed all over them. "Come on. We have this last segment to tape and then we'll be done." The three women walked out of the room, leaving Zach behind to change.

It was nearly 4:00 p.m. and Zach and Kelly had been taping for almost two hours. Though he'd expected some uneasiness on Kelly's part, especially after the intimate moments they'd shared in her hotel room that morning, she'd been the consummate professional. No one would have guessed that they slept in the same bed last night or that he'd brought her to a powerful orgasm that morning.

Thoughts of her had occupied his mind from the very second he'd awakened in her bed until the time she arrived at the station. Though he hadn't put his finger on the cause of this minor obsession, he suspected it was rooted in the contradictions he found in this woman.

One moment, she was cool, aloof and untouchable, and then the next she was a sultry-eyed seductress. She was nervous then confident, shy then aggressive, serious then silly. Her emotions seemed to turn on a dime and Zach wasn't sure what to expect from moment to moment. Seducing her had been a challenge, but one he was more than willing to accept.

He changed into the boxers, then turned back to the mirror. Raking his hands through his hair, he deliberately disrupted the careful work that Jane had put in with her combs and sprays. If they wanted a twenty-four-year-old, then that's what they'd get. He rubbed the narrow trail of hair on his chest. Maybe he should have shaved his chest.

"Zach! Come on. We're ready for you."

He glanced over to see Jane peeking in the door. "Do you think this is all right?" he asked, pointing to his chest.

She sighed dramatically and walked into the room, then grabbed his hand. "You look fine. This skit isn't about you, it's about her, the older woman. You're just eye candy."

"Gee, thanks," he muttered.

When he got out to the set, he sat down on the edge of the bed. Familiar territory, but strangely enough, he felt a little uneasy. After all, just eight hours before, he and Kelly had been curled up in her hotel room, sharing a bed not much different than this one. And he no longer had to imagine what she looked like without her clothes, as he'd enjoyed that view, as well.

What if the reality of the situation began to creep in and he couldn't help but get...aroused? How embarrassing would that be to pitch a tent in his boxers, right in front of his coworkers?

"All right," Nicole said. "Where's Kelly?"

"Here I am." She stepped out of the shadows on the right side of the set and walked to the bed.

Zach swallowed a groan when he saw her, dressed in a silky camisole and skimpy shorts that revealed her belly and the sweet curves of her buttocks. She might as well have been wearing nothing because he knew exactly what was hidden beneath the clinging fabric. Zach quickly grabbed a pillow and put it over his lap.

"All right," Nicole said. "We're going to start with the two of you lying in bed. It's a Sunday morning, you've had a hot night in bed together and this is the aftermath of sex with a younger man. Zach, after the first five seconds, I want you to turn your full attention on Kelly. I want you to be sexy and playful, try to distract her from her newspaper. Kelly, I need you to make it clear that you're not interested. Difficult as it may seem, you don't want to have sex eight times a day with this boy. We're trying to illustrate the differences between the sex drives here. This will lead into Eve's discussion of the staying power of younger men."

"What about our lines?" Kelly asked.

"We've made some changes in the script. Actually, there won't be a script for this, we're going to put music under it. It's meant to be playful."

"But I learned my lines," Zach said.

"Well, now you won't have to say anything. Kelly, we

want you reading the *New York Times*. And, Zach, we want
you playing with this." Nicole handed him a Game Boy.

Zach frowned. "I haven't played with one of these for
years."

"I know. But it's just a prop. We want to show the differences between you two."

"No," Zach said. "This will make me look like an idiot.
Twenty-four-year-old guys play Halo on a plasma screen,
we don't play with Game Boys. And that Game Boy is at
least six years old. Any guy my age would know that.
Besides, on a Sunday morning, I'm reading the *New York
Times,* too."

"I think they're just trying to make a visual statement
that conveys the difference in our maturity levels," Kelly
explained.

"I know what they're trying to do," Zach said. "They're
trying to make it look like all younger guys sleeping with
older women are brainless. That they have nothing to offer
but a good time in the sack and a pretty face to escort her
around town. I liked the script the way it was. We talked
to each other."

Nicole stared at him through narrowed eyes. "Don't
give me trouble on this, Zach. We're almost finished. Let's
just wrap this up and go home."

"Then don't make me look stupid," he said.

"It's not you," Kelly whispered. "You're playing a part.
This isn't about you, it's about the characters."

Zach stood up, still holding the pillow in front of him. "I
can't work like this," he said. "It's not going to happen."

He walked back to the dressing room, closed the door behind him and sat down in one of the makeup chairs, kicking his bare feet up on the counter. He peeked beneath the pillow and cursed softly. If Nicole wanted to illustrate how a twenty-four-year-old guy could get a boner just thinking about a beautiful woman, then he'd be the perfect guy to play the part.

A soft knock sounded on the door and he put the pillow back in place. No doubt Nicole was coming in to rip him a new one. At least he wouldn't have to worry about his erection. He'd be soft in a matter of minutes. But it wasn't Nicole who slipped inside, it was Kelly.

She looked so sexy, her hair falling around her face, dressed in her tiny little pajamas. The erection that had sprung to life the moment she walked into the room had no chance of abating now, Zach mused. In fact, it was growing harder.

"What is your problem?"

Zach tossed the pillow aside and pointed to his crotch.

Kelly's eyes went wide. "Oh," she murmured, wincing. "I didn't realize. When did that happen?"

"The minute I saw you in that getup. I started thinking about this morning and one thing led to another and I got hard. Are you wearing any underwear beneath that?"

"No," Kelly said. "The bra straps would show and I didn't want panty lines."

"Thank you for that," Zach muttered. "Maybe if you would have come out wearing flannel pajamas, I might have stood a chance."

"Older women don't always wear flannel pajamas. I wear sexy stuff to bed sometimes." She pointed to his crotch. "That's why you put up the fuss about the script?"

"No. I made a fuss because it's an unrealistic scene. I''ve worked on enough films to know. If you were in bed with a sixteen-year-old, then the Game Boy would probably work. It just doesn't fit my character. Not the way he's been developed in the first three segments."

"It's just a little skit."

"Yeah, and who knows who's going to see me in it. Once it's on tape, it's out there forever. Someday, I'll be pitching my new blockbuster on Letterman and they'll trot this out and I'll have to watch it in front of millions of people."

"I don't think that's going to happen," Kelly said.

"You don't think I'll ever be on Letterman? Or you don't think I'll ever direct a blockbuster?"

"Can't you just do this for me?" She jumped up to sit on the counter, placing her hand on his calf and smoothing it back and forth. "You know, experienced Hollywood actors sometimes have that same problem when they're doing a sex scene. It's nothing to be embarrassed about."

"I work with those women. They're going to think I'm some kind of pervert."

"Well, then, you have to find a way to keep it from happening. Get an image in your head, something that you don't find sexy at all. Pretend you're having sex with your aunt Mildred or your high-school chemistry teacher."

"She was really hot," Zach said. "And I don't have an

aunt Mildred. My mother was an only child and my father had three brothers."

"Well, there must be something."

"It would be a lot easier if you weren't in the room with me," Zach said. "And what makes it even more difficult is what we did this morning. I keep thinking about that and it gets me going. Hell, I haven't *stopped* thinking about sex since you walked into the studio yesterday. You know, if you wouldn't have dropped that towel, I probably would have left and not even thought about doing what I did."

"You're blaming this on me?" Kelly asked.

"Entirely on you," Zach replied.

She shook her head and jumped off the counter, then began to pace back and forth behind him. "This is exactly why they tell you not to get involved with your leading men," Kelly said. "It always causes problems."

"You've caused this problem before?" Zach asked.

"No! I'm just saying problems in general." She stopped pacing. "I know. Think of the most awful, horrible, humiliating experience you've ever had with a woman. Close your eyes," she ordered. "Go ahead, do it. Focus."

Zach did as ordered. It didn't take a lot of thought to come up with the worst experience in his life. It was the day he got kicked out of film school. Well, technically, he hadn't been kicked out, or even asked to leave. He had been told his grant had not been extended for the spring semester, which meant no money to live on and no way to pay tuition.

That had been the worst day of his life and it had all been

brought on by his penchant for messing around with older women. He'd made the mistake of bedding an older woman who held control over his post-graduate education. Though she wasn't the dean of cinema studies at the film school, she was a dean in the school of arts and humanities and powerful enough to turn his life upside down just to spite him.

They'd met at a cocktail reception for one of his instructors whose film had been nominated for an award at Sundance. She was smart and beautiful and recently divorced and had spent most of the evening flirting with him. They'd gone home to her apartment and spent that night and the next day in bed. It was only later that he learned who she really was.

She'd insisted that it didn't make a difference, that they were both adults and no matter what happened between them, it wouldn't have an impact on his education. She'd lied. When it came time to end it, she'd been angry and bitter and took it out on him. He probably could have sued, but in truth, he'd been as culpable as she had. And he'd accepted it as his punishment for taking such a silly risk with his future.

"See, it's working already."

He blinked, brought out of his thoughts to his present predicament. Zach glanced down to see that Kelly was correct. "I guess it is," he murmured.

"What were you thinking about?"

"Dead bunnies," he replied.

She wrinkled her nose. "Ewwww." Kelly leaned up against the counter and met his gaze. "So we can finish this?"

"I'm not going to do the thing with the Game Boy."

"Nicole said we can do the original version." She sighed and stared at him for a long moment. "You didn't want to finish this, did you? You thought if you caused another delay they'd make me stick around another day. I have a ticket back to L.A. tomorrow. I'm going to be on that plane, Zach."

With a curse, Zach stood up. "All right. Fine, we'll finish it."

Were his motives that transparent? Hell, he didn't want to think about Kelly walking out of his life—at least not so quickly. He wanted more time to explore this fascination he had with her. Once again, he'd gotten himself mixed up with an older woman, but this time, there was a balance to the power. She'd go back to L.A. and continue on with her life as if she'd never met him, and he'd stay here and try to forget about her. No harm, no foul.

"So, we're having dinner tonight, right?"

"If that will get you back on the set, then yes, we're having dinner tonight."

Zach smiled. "It's a deal." He followed her back out onto the set, jumped onto the bed and stretched out beneath the covers. Kelly joined him, pulling the sheet up to her waist. It was a small victory, but he'd take it. And who knows where dinner might lead?

"Are we ready?" Nicole asked.

He snuggled a bit closer to Kelly and sighed. "I'm ready."

"I'm ready," Kelly said.

"Then let's go with the original version," Nicole conceded, sending Zach a pointed glare. "No Game Boy, just dialogue."

"Dead bunnies," Zach whispered beneath his breath as he felt her naked thigh brush against his. "Dead bunnies, dead bunnies, pots of dead bunnies simmering on the stove."

Once he had Kelly alone again, there was sure to be a way to convince her to stay for a few more days. Though he couldn't always control his crotch, he was a master at charming women. He'd find just the right words to make her want to spend the next week in his bed.

WHAT DID ONE WEAR to a seduction? The question had plagued Kelly ever since she had arrived back at the hotel. She and Zach had finished filming at five and by the time she'd left the studio she was exhausted—not from hard work but from trying to maintain her composure.

It was difficult to be professional when all she wanted to do was help Zach out of his boxer shorts and attend to his little problem. Every time he looked at her, all she could think about was what they'd shared that morning, what he'd done to her body and what he'd made her feel. And what they might share that evening, once alone in her hotel room. After all, at this point in their relationship, *dinner* was just a polite euphemism for sex, wasn't it?

A knock sounded on her room door and Kelly glanced at her watch. They'd agreed on dinner at seven and it was barely six. She still hadn't dried her hair or put on makeup.

Clutching her robe over her breasts, Kelly walked to the door. "Go away. You're early."

"Miss Castelle?"

Kelly peered through the peephole. A bellman stood on the other side. She unlocked the door and opened it and he held out a pale pink bag. Kelly recognized the logo from Sweet Nothings, Angie's lingerie shop.

"This was delivered to the front desk a few minutes ago," the bellman said.

"Thank you." Kelly took the bag from him, then hurried into the room to grab a tip from her purse. When she was alone, she dumped the contents of the bag onto the bed and picked through the pretty tissue paper to find a sexy push-up bra and a matching thong, both in black. A note had been scrawled on a gift card.

"'I thought you might need these,'" Kelly read. "'Just in case. Love, Angie.'" La Perla. She'd never been able to afford designer lingerie on an actress's salary but it wasn't difficult to see why so many women in L.A. were La Perla addicts.

The bra fit beautifully and it looked like a dream with its sheer straps and sides and intricate ruching on the cups. And the thong was just a wisp of fabric, meant to tantalize and tempt. They were almost too pretty to cover with clothes, and Kelly considered opening the door in just her lingerie. There'd certainly be no doubt about what she wanted from Zach then.

She walked into the bathroom to dry her hair, contemplating her first move. They only had one night together, so it wouldn't do to waste time with formalities, silly chitchat and a discussion of where they might go for dinner. She'd order dinner from room service. That would send a subtle message that she wasn't interested in an evening out.

Kelly switched on the hair dryer and bent over at the waist. She'd be confident but coy, no nervousness like she'd experienced the night before. It was clear that Zach wanted her, and in the end, she'd give him whatever he wanted, however he wanted it. A shiver skittered down her spine. If she had any thoughts of holding on to her sexual inhibitions, she needed to put those aside right now.

She switched off the hair dryer, then grabbed the phone, punching in the number for room service. "I'd like to order dinner," she said. "Room twelve fifteen."

"What would you like, Miss Castelle?"

"I don't know. Anything. You choose."

There was silence on the other end of the line. "I—I'm afraid we don't do that for the guests," the woman said. "There's a menu in your room."

"Steak," she said. "And French fries and some kind of salad. And pie for dessert. Apple or cherry would be good."

"How would you like the steak?"

"Medium rare," she said. "Better send up two steaks. Make one medium. Oh, and a bottle of red wine. No, make that champagne."

She'd have to put the meal on her credit card. The show would never spring for the champagne. But a hundred-dollar steak dinner was worth it for one night of hot sex with a guy like Zach.

Kelly looked at herself in the mirror and for a moment she didn't recognize the woman she saw, the woman with the expensive underwear and the tousled hair, the bright eyes and high color in her cheeks. She felt wicked and sexy and alive, as if she'd stepped outside of her own life for a little while to enjoy something decadent and forbidden.

Why not take a chance? There was nothing wrong with indulging in all her desires for just one night. What happened in this room would be the stuff of fantasies. There would be nothing off-limits, nothing she wouldn't try if asked. And what harm could it possibly do? She'd leave town tomorrow and never see Zach again. There would be nothing to remind her of her wild night in Atlanta, except the memories. Somehow, Kelly knew that sex with Zach would be impossible to forget.

She decided to greet him wearing only her robe. After all, he'd seen her in something much more skimpy that afternoon. And she wanted to leave something to the imagination. It was part of a long seduction to undress each other. Kelly tied the sash tightly around her waist and pulled the lapels together. But as she sat and waited on the end of the bed, she carefully arranged the front of the robe so that it gaped open slightly.

At exactly 7:00 p.m., another knock sounded at the door. She took a deep breath and walked over to open it. Her hand trembled slightly as she reached for the knob and she clenched her fingers together. Then, with another deep breath, she pulled the door open.

Zach stood on the other side, wearing a crisp blue

shirt, untucked at the waist and sleeves rolled to the elbow, a pair of khaki pants and sandals. The instant he saw her, a cocky grin curled the corners of his mouth. "Hey, there," he murmured.

"Hi," she said. Kelly stepped aside, and he walked into the room.

He turned to gaze at her. "What? No flannel pajamas?"

Kelly giggled. "I have a pair in my suitcase, if you'd like me to put them on."

"No, that wouldn't be a good idea." He waited as she crossed to him, then reached out and fingered the lapel of her bathrobe, revealing a bit more of her lacy bra. A shiver skittered down her spine at his touch.

"Nice," he murmured.

Kelly glanced up at him and met his gaze, seeing the blatant desire in his eyes. "I thought we'd have dinner in the room," she said. "I—I'm really exhausted and I just didn't feel like going out."

"Oh, I'm exhausted, too," he said with an easy grin. "So what did you have in mind for our evening in?"

Kelly shrugged. "I don't know. A little Game Boy. Maybe we could read the paper together, watch some sports on TV. Have a few beers? Isn't that what guys like you enjoy?"

Zach shook his head, then grabbed her by the waist and pulled her against him. "Would you like me to show you what guys like me enjoy?"

"I guess it couldn't hurt," she said.

"I promise, it won't hurt." He reached down and untied

her robe, then brushed it aside. He smoothed his hands over her chest, his fingers dancing across her skin. Goose bumps prickled on her arms and Kelly watched his hands as she enjoyed his touch.

He leaned forward, as if to kiss her, but then didn't, his lips just inches from hers, his breath warm on her skin. Every time he leaned toward her, she waited, but then he drew away, as if teasing her, challenging her to take the lead.

Kelly had never purposely seduced a man in her life, never taken the role of the aggressor. But there were no rules anymore. Everything she knew about sex was null and void, the expiration date long past. If Zach wanted her to possess him, then that's what she'd do.

She grabbed the front of his shirt and yanked the two sides apart, a button flying over her shoulder as she did, exposing his chest. Zach chuckled and she glanced up, smiling at him, pleased with herself. She brushed the shirt off his shoulders and it dropped to the floor behind him. Then she began a careful exploration of his neck and collarbone, dropping wet kisses from his ear to his shoulder.

"I've been thinking about this all day long," he murmured. "About touching you. Tasting you again." Zach cupped her face in his hands and tried to kiss her, but she pulled back and smiled. "Oh, you want to play that game?" he asked.

Kelly nodded, then watched as he reached for the tie of her robe, and slowly pulled it out of the loops, then waved it in front of her. "If you want me to keep my hands off of you, then you're going to have to do something about it."

"You want me to tie you up?" she asked.

"Whatever works."

Kelly snatched the tie from his hands, then slowly circled him. When she stood behind him, she grabbed his wrists and gently wrapped the sash around them, securing it with a loose bow. Then she shrugged out of her robe and tossed it onto the bed.

When she came back around, dressed only in the lingerie, Kelly heard him suck in a sharp breath. She laughed softly as she ran her fingertips down his chest, scraping softly with her nails. "Now what?" she asked.

"Now you have your way with me."

"Oh, that won't take much work," she teased, emboldened by the little game he'd started.

"No?"

Kelly reached out and dragged his shirt over his shoulders until it tangled around his wrists. Then, she undid his belt, letting her hand brush across the front of his trousers. "What are you thinking about now?" she asked.

"Definitely not bunnies," he murmured, his voice raw with desire.

Kelly bent down and removed his sandals, then unzipped his pants. They slipped down to his hips and she smiled when she saw the sexy white boxer briefs that he wore. "I think we need to get you completely naked," she said.

As she grabbed the waistband of his briefs and pulled them down over his hips, she realized how easily she'd already been swept into the fantasy. She wasn't embarrassed or inhibited at all with their teasing. Instead, he'd simply introduced her to a new kind of foreplay, one that was silly and spontaneous.

When he was naked, she stepped back and let her gaze take in the details of his body. He was beautiful, there was no disputing that fact, all hard muscle and smooth skin, lean and lithe like an athlete.

"What are you going to do with me?" he asked.

Kelly stepped back and sat on the edge of the bed. "I think I'll just look for a little while." She leaned back, bracing her arms behind her, and sent him a smug smile. "You're a very handsome man."

"You have to touch me," he said.

She shook her head. "No, I don't."

"You're just going to make me stand here?"

Kelly sighed dramatically, then reached behind her and unhooked her bra. She threw it at him and it fell on his shoulder. Then she stood and shimmied out of her panties and tossed those his way. They landed on his feet.

She fixed her gaze on his shaft and smiled. Slowly, it grew harder as she began to smooth her hands over her body. Zach moaned softly, still bound by the no-touching rule of their game. "See?" she murmured. "I don't need to touch you."

"You're making me crazy," he said.

"I know. And it's fun." Kelly got off the bed and knelt down in front of him, his erection brushing against her cheek. She kissed the tip of his shaft, then slowly ran her tongue down to the base and up again. She leaned into him, reaching around to untie his wrists.

The instant he was free, he grabbed her and pulled her to her feet, his mouth coming down on hers. He seemed almost frantic to touch her, his hands skimming over her body and drawing her against him. With each kiss and caress, he silently invited her to come with him, to lose herself in this hazy world of passion they'd created. Kelly made a note to thank Angie for the lingerie. It had obviously done the trick, making her feel quite naughty and making him hard with desire.

He stumbled back toward the bed, dragging her with him until they fell onto the mattress. His hands immediately moved to her breasts, teasing at her nipples with his thumbs until they were hard. Kelly tipped her head back and let the warm desire pulse through her veins. Reaching up, she wrapped her arms around his neck and guided his lips to her breasts.

Zach took her nipple into his mouth, gently sucking, cupping her flesh in his hands. At the same time, she reached down and began to stroke him, slowly at first, her fingers wrapped tightly around his heat. His abdomen tensed until she could make out every muscle and he held his breath, as if he were dancing on the edge of release.

And then, he grabbed her wrists and pinned them over her head, rolling on top of her. He pressed his hips into hers, then pulled her thigh up his leg. Kelly was amazed at how perfectly they fit together. Gazing down into her eyes, he began to move against her, rocking gently, his shaft rubbing against the slit between her legs.

She shifted and his movement brought a flood of sensation, and a soft moan escaped her lips. Suddenly, she couldn't think clearly. Every movement brought another wave of pleasure, each building on the last, bringing her closer to the edge.

Sex had always been so complicated in the past, filled with meaning that Kelly couldn't quite grasp, tinged with doubts and insecurities that she didn't want to examine. But with Zach, everything was simple—hunger and release, hunger and release.

"I want you inside me," she murmured. Never once had she demanded anything of a man in bed. But with Zach, she was free to express her needs. He wouldn't judge her or question her request. From the moment they'd first been intimate, Kelly knew that his only wish was to please her.

She pointed to the bedside table and he stood up and opened the drawer, finding the boxes of condoms inside. He tore one packet from the string of three, then handed it to her. Sitting up, she opened it. Then, she put the tip of the condom between her lips.

"What are you doing?" he asked, chuckling softly.

"I saw this in movie once," she replied. Leaning forward, she placed the condom on the tip of his shaft and then, unrolled it along his length with her lips, taking him deep into her mouth.

Zach groaned. "Oh, my God."

"It works," Kelly said with a satisfied smile.

"I'd assume this wasn't a G-rated movie?"

"No, it was a porno," she said, smoothing the condom

down the rest of the way with her fingers. "I was up for a part as a call girl and I needed to do some research."

"I sure hope you didn't have to display this little talent at the audition," he said.

Kelly leaned back, bracing herself on her elbows. "I never even got to read. I walked into the casting session and they rejected me right away. I didn't look the part."

He furrowed his fingers through her hair, then crawled back on the bed to lie beside her. "A seductress, yes. A call girl, no. There's just something about you that's…untouchable."

"I lost my virginity years ago," she said.

"It's not about that. It's like you hold a part of yourself back, a part that no man can have. And that's why they want you, because it's there and they can't have it."

"Men don't want me," Kelly amended.

"Yes, they do. They're just afraid to try and then fail. Because then they'd realize just what they'd lost."

"And you aren't afraid to try?"

Zach shook his head. "No. You're worth the risk."

Kelly reached out and touched his cheek with her hand. He leaned over her and his tongue teased at her mouth, tracing along her lower lip until it was damp with the taste of him. Then he covered her mouth with his and kissed her, deeply, completely, and there was no longer any need for games. They'd both been stripped bare and now it was only lust that drove them forward.

He wasn't afraid to want her, to need her. And when he slowly pushed inside of her, Kelly realized she wasn't afraid to want him. She closed her eyes as he buried himself, filling her completely.

Zach was right. She had always held a part of herself back, knowing that to give herself completely to a man would be far too great a risk. Back in L.A., her life had become all about compromise, but here things were different. She was starting fresh, without all the disappointments of the past to weigh her down. She could be seductive and uninhibited and hedonistic without consequence or regret.

Zach began to move inside her and she moaned softly, raking her fingers through his hair, her desire building as he plunged deeper with each stroke. Time seemed to slow as her body reacted to his and she lost herself in a haze of intense sensation.

When he pulled her on top of him, she felt every inch of him deep inside of her, the connection unbreakable and unyielding. Kelly arched back, her desire spiraling out of control as she rocked above him.

"Look at me."

She opened her eyes and stared down at Zach. He was beautiful…perfect…everything a woman might want in a sexual conquest.

"Don't move," he whispered.

She did as he asked and he slipped his hand between them and began to caress her, teasing until she felt the slow ascent to her release begin. It was as if he could read her responses and he slowly withdrew, then slipped inside of her. She was completely focused on his touch, on the feel of him moving and the sensations that coursed through her body.

And then, she was there. She cried out as he took her over the edge, her gaze fixed on his. A moment later, he joined her, finding his end deep inside of her body. It was perfect, it was complete and it was like nothing she'd ever experienced before.

A knock sounded on the door. "That must be dinner," Kelly murmured, raking her hands through her hair. She bent over him and her hair fell about his face as she kissed him. "I ordered steak."

"You are the perfect woman," Zach teased.

She hopped off the bed and grabbed her robe, then slipped it over her naked body. "You'd better put some pants on," she said.

Zach watched her as she grabbed the tie for her robe and wrapped it around her waist. This would all vanish in a matter of hours, this world they'd created. But she would enjoy it while it lasted. And later, she'd remember every single moment of her time spent with this man, a man who had transformed her into a different woman for just one exquisite night.

ZACH SAT IN THE high-backed office chair, his hands linked behind his head. The lights were low in the editing suite and he'd wandered in after they'd finished taping the day's show. Jeff had been working on the offline editing for the footage with Kelly, going through all the tape and picking out the best takes. Later, the footage would be uploaded onto the computer and edited into the planned segments.

He hadn't seen Kelly in six or seven hours, not since they'd said their goodbyes at the door of her hotel room. Both of them had been exhausted, spending the entire night enjoying the pleasures of the flesh. They'd slept for an hour or two and then parted. There'd been no exchange of phone numbers, no promises to keep in touch. What they'd shared last night had begun and ended in her bed and now it was over.

Zach had indulged in a number of one-night stands in the past and had never felt an ounce of regret. They were what they were supposed to be—physical gratification without any expectations. In every case, he and his partner had gotten exactly what they'd wanted out of the encounter.

But now, even though he'd gone into this brief affair with open eyes, he felt as if he'd left something unfinished or unfulfilled, as if there might have been more between the two of them. Even while sharing a final kiss, he'd been torn. He'd wanted to ask her to stay, to find some way to tempt her. But Kelly had made it clear she was returning to Los Angeles on a late morning flight—end of discussion. She had her own life and he wasn't a part of it.

"How did you get talked in to doing this?" Jeff asked, pointing at the monitor.

"I volunteered," Zach said, leaning forward. He grabbed his can of Dr Pepper and took a long swallow, staring at the beautiful image on the screen.

What was it about her that had drawn him in? Yes, she was stunning, but there had been something else. From the moment he'd first seen her, he'd written her off as a woman completely out of his league, unattainable. His flirtation had been all in good fun. And when she'd responded, he'd been surprised.

Now, as he looked her, he remembered her naked, lying in his arms, her dark hair spread across his shoulder, her cheek warm against his chest. They'd been so close for those moments—the moment she dissolved into her release, the moment he'd lost himself inside of her. And now, Zach had to wonder if it had all been just a dream.

"Yeah, I would have volunteered, too," Jeff murmured. "She's hot."

Zach nodded. "Hey, you think anyone would mind if I made a dub of the raw footage?"

Jeff glanced over at him. "Well, I'm really not sup-posed to—" He hesitated. "Just don't say anything, all right?" Jeff handed him the B roll and Zach slid his chair over to the dubbing decks. He threw in an empty VHS tape and popped the half-inch tape into the top deck, then hit Play and Record.

The door to the editing suite swung open and Cole Crawford stood in the shaft of light from the hall. "Hey, Zach. You interested in stopping by Latitude for a drink after work? The girls are going to a friend's house for dinner right from school, so I'm free and single for the night."

Zach glanced over at the tape deck, knowing that Cole would not approve of raw video leaving the studio. "I can't.

I've got a meeting tonight with the guys from ESPN. I'm freelancing as a cameraman for the Falcons preseason games and I'm on the schedule for the game next Thursday night."

"Can you get me tickets?"

"I can try," Zach said. "There are usually some comps floating around. I'll see what I can do."

Cole was the supervising producer with the show and a single father of twin seven-year-old daughters, Susan and Schuyler. He and Zach had become good friends since Cole had hired him last February and they occasionally went out after work for a beer at their local watering hole, Latitude 33.

Zach didn't have many friends in Atlanta and it was nice to have a guy he could count on, even if that guy was a family man with kids.

Cole wandered inside and pulled up a chair, his gaze fixed on the monitor. "I've been hearing about your segment," he said.

"From who?"

"All the women in this place. Nicole, Jane, Eve. They were all in here this morning watching the footage while they were drinking their lattes. They seem to think you've got a future in front of the camera."

"I don't think so," Zach said, shaking his head. "I'd rather direct."

"I don't know," Cole responded as they continued to watch the tape of the bedroom scene, "looks like you could have cut the sexual tension there with a knife."

"I was acting," Zach said.

"Exactly my point. You're pretty good at it."

"I've spent enough time behind the camera to know what works and what doesn't."

Cole shrugged. "Maybe," he murmured. "Hell, she is really beautiful. What's her name?"

"Kelly Castelle," Zach said.

"Where did Nicole find her?"

"She's from Los Angeles."

"Too bad. It would be nice to think a woman like that lived in Atlanta. If she did, you could have invited her for drinks with us and introduced her to me. This is the kind of woman I need to find, someone a little older, more settled, interested in raising two daughters."

"Once we're both millionaires, I'm sure we'll have women swarming all over us," Zach said.

"Yeah. Maybe. Did Nicole tell you we heard from Liza's lawyer this morning?"

"I missed the production meeting," Zach said. "I was late getting into work."

"Oversleep?" Cole asked.

Zach gave him a sideways glance and smiled. "Yeah. Busy night last night."

"Did you spend your evening with her?" Cole asked, pointing at the screen.

Chuckling, Zach shook his head. "Hey, a gentleman never kisses and tells. Besides, she's on her way back to L.A. It was just one of those things. Chemistry, that's all."

"On screen and off," Cole said, smiling.

"It was pretty amazing," Zach admitted. "I mean, one day I'm standing behind the camera, doing my job, and that beautiful creature steps in front of the lens and I can't take my eyes off of her." He drew a deep breath, pushing images of Kelly from his head. "So, what's going on with the lawsuit?"

Zach hadn't thought twice about putting money into the Lot'o'Bucks pool when he started working for the show. He liked to gamble occasionally and the baseball and football pools amongst the crew at *Just Between Us* hadn't started yet. He'd thought it would be a good way to get to know his coworkers, to join in the fun.

To his shock, they'd hit the big money just a few months after he'd started contributing. Thirty-eight million. The sum was almost too much to comprehend. Between Eve, Cole, Jane, Nicole and himself, each share was worth seven and a half million, four million after taxes. But the payout had been stopped dead in its tracks when Liza Skinner, a former employee, decided she wanted a share.

Liza had worked for the station and always been a part of the lottery group. But she'd left the station a year before the winning ticket had been purchased and she suddenly re-appeared, claiming that she deserved her share. The others disputed her claim, saying that only those who contributed to the ticket would share in the winnings.

"Jenna Hamilton gave Liza the offer to settle," Cole said, "and she turned it down."

"Why? How can she think she has a claim after all this time?"

· "She and Jane and Eve have been friends for years. They started together on the show and then, after she quit, the show took off. Maybe she felt she could just walk back in and everything would be the same, that we owed her something for all her hard work."

"I guess I can understand her point," Zach said. "She had contributed a whole lot more to the pool than either Nicole or me. She should have just accepted the settlement. If it goes to court, she could get nothing."

"Well, part of her case still rests on the fact that we continued to play her number and that she had paid ahead. That makes it look like she was in the pool."

"How long is this going to go on?" Zach asked.

"I don't know. I could really use this money."

"It's a lot of money," Zach said.

Funny how he'd already started spending it. When he'd come to Atlanta he was desperate for a job that would pay the rent and now he'd get a check for 7.6 million dollars. After taxes, he'd probably have more than enough to finance his own film—or to go back to City University and finish his degree without the need for a grant.

But if Liza took a share, then they'd all have to give up 1.6 million dollars. To Zach, he'd be happy with what was left. Six million was still a lot of money, three million for him and three for Uncle Sam. He could make a really nice film for three million dollars.

"It's hard to put it all in perspective," Zach said. "We're talking millions. I can't really comprehend how much that is. The most I've ever had in my wallet at one time has been a couple hundred bucks."

"It will change our lives," Cole murmured.

Their names had been all over the media, their photos splashed across the pages of the local papers. Yet Zach had managed to remain fairly anonymous. But he understood that having millions would make him a target for gold-digging women. He had to wonder if it might have altered Kelly's opinion of him. She may not have considered a future relationship with a lowly cameraman. But if he'd told her he was about to become a multimillionaire, it might have been a whole different story.

There was no use second-guessing himself now. She was gone, out of his life forever and he'd have to put his passion for her in the past. Four million would go a long way to keeping his thoughts occupied with other things.

Cole stood up. "Well, I guess it's bottled beer and a frozen dinner for me tonight," he said. "I'll see you guys tomorrow."

Zach waved at him and a few minutes after he left, he pushed his chair back and grabbed the dub of the B roll he'd made. Jeff handed him the A roll and he made a dub of that, then took both tapes and headed to the door. "Thanks," he said, holding up the tapes.

"No problem," Jeff replied. "Enjoy."

Zach grabbed his messenger bag from his cubicle near the production office, then headed to the door, tucking the tapes safely inside. If he knew what was good for him, he'd go home and shower and then head out to a bar and find female companionship for the night. There was no better way to forget a beautiful woman than with another beautiful woman. It had worked in the past. But tonight was going to be different. Tonight, he planned to sit back, have a few beers and enjoy reliving his time with Kelly.

4

"WHAT DO YOU THINK of this?" Angie asked, holding up a pale green bustier, edged in cream-colored satin. "I loved the color, and the fabric just feels like a dream. I have these on automatic reorder. I know they're going to just fly out the door."

"Fly out the door," Kelly repeated.

"Don't worry," Angie said with a smile. "You'll get to know the merchandise over time and then you'll know exactly what the customers want. It's not that difficult."

"I still haven't decided whether this will be a permanent move," Kelly said.

"I'm allowed to be optimistic," Angie said. "After all, I managed to talk you out of taking that flight back to L.A., didn't I? And you've learned how to run the register at the shop and take inventory and check in merchandise. Before long, I'll be sending you to New York on buying trips."

"I appreciate your faith in me," Kelly said.

Angie threw her arm around Kelly's shoulders and gave her a hug. "I'm just so glad to have my best friend back. I didn't realize how much I missed having a best friend. When I moved here, I came for Joe. I've had a hard time meeting people who really understood me. I guess I have too much L.A. left inside to become a proper Southern girl."

"Then I'll never fit in," Kelly said.

"We'll be outcasts together!" Angie got to her feet and walked across the storeroom to an empty rack filled with plastic hangers. She grabbed a handful and returned to her spot on the floor next to Kelly.

"Have you called him yet?" she asked as she put a bra-and-panty set onto the store's signature black hangers.

"Who?"

"Don't play dumb," Angie said. "You know who I'm talking about. Your little friend. Zach Haas."

"My little friend?"

"You know what I mean," Angie teased.

She'd been in Atlanta for a week and Kelly had thought about calling Zach every waking moment of every day. It had taken every ounce of her willpower not to pick up the phone and invite him to "dinner." "No, I haven't called him. There's no need. What happened between us is over. It was just a casual thing. A one-night stand."

Angie studied her for a long moment, her gaze suspicious. "Are you sure? If you enjoyed one night, why not try two or three. Or thirty-six."

"If I'm going to stay in Atlanta and build a new life here, I have to know it's for the right reasons. And staying because I think there might be a future with Zach Haas would be the wrong reason. So it's better not to go there."

"All right," Angie said. "I just think you should keep

all your options open—professionally, emotionally and sexually."

Kelly reached in to the box and grabbed another lingerie set, unwrapping it from the tissue paper. "I'm going to take one day at a time."

"Is there anything you need? I know the condo just has the bare necessities. We can go out shopping after work. Joe is picking up Caroline from preschool this afternoon and taking her to swimming lessons."

"You've already done so much for me," Kelly said. Angie had lent her a few pretty sundresses and given her an advance on her first week's salary, enough to fill out her wardrobe until she went back to L.A. She'd also given her a choice of lingerie off the clearance rack. And Joe had offered Kelly a lovely rent-free condo just a few miles from the store, a furnished one-bedroom that his company kept for visiting executives. Together, they were determined to convince Kelly to relocate to Atlanta and she was beginning to think it might be the right move.

She loved working at the Buckhead store, learning the merchandise, meeting the regular customers, helping Angie plan the decor for the new shop in midtown. She could make a career of this and be very happy and never have to worry about where the next job might come from and how much it would pay.

It was a big decision to let go of her dreams. But the longer she stayed out of L.A., the more she began to realize she had been living in denial for years. The chances of making it in Hollywood had been slim at best. And after all this time, no one really knew her.

Women her age didn't suddenly make themselves a career. They continued a career that began in their late teens or early twenties. Jennifer, Julia, Reese, they'd all become well-known when they were young and now that they were over thirty, they were able to make their own choices. She didn't have that luxury.

Diane, Angie's afternoon salesclerk, poked her head in the door of the storeroom. "My shift ends in a few minutes and I've got to leave to pick up the boys from school. Can one of you cover the register until six?"

Kelly scrambled to her feet. "I'll watch the front," she said.

Angie stood and grabbed the last of the lingerie from the box, placing it on a nearby table. "And I should probably get going. If we're not going to shop, then I think I'll make a nice homemade dinner for my family. Joe's mother gave me her recipe for macaroni and cheese. It's a heart attack on a plate, but it's Joe's favorite."

"You're cooking?" Kelly asked, giggling at the notion of Angie in a kitchen. Her old roommate used to exist on Jack in the Box cheeseburgers and Fresca. The only time she went into the kitchen of their apartment was to retrieve a can of soda from the refrigerator.

"Would you like to come for dinner?"

Kelly shook her head. "No, I'm just going to settle in for the night. I have to call my agent before she leaves for the day."

"All right. We'll finish this tomorrow morning." Angie gave Kelly a hug. "I just can't believe you're here. You know I'll do anything to get you to stay."

"I know," Kelly said. She watched as Angie gathered her things and slipped out the back door of the shop. Then she flipped the dead bolt on the door and walked to the front of the store.

As she passed each rack, she carefully sized the merchandise and faced the hangers forward. She passed the rack that held a black bra-and-thong set, the same style she'd worn that night with Zach. Kelly picked it up and fingered the sheer fabric and the intricate ruching, remembering the very moment that she'd taken it off and thrown it at him. An image of his naked body swirled in her head and she smiled.

The memory of that night was still so vivid in her mind. They'd been wild for each other, making love into the early hours of the morning, then falling into an exhausted sleep. They'd overslept and said a hasty goodbye, Zach late for a production meeting at the studio.

In truth, Kelly was glad they hadn't lingered over their farewells. She didn't want any promises to stay in touch or plans to see each other in the future. Their affair was just that, something with a beginning and an end.

Still, that didn't stop her from thinking about him, about the night they spent together, about what might happen if they spent another night in bed. She'd never considered herself a very sexual being, but she'd obviously never met the right man. Zach had brought something out in her that had been hidden—or maybe it hadn't existed before.

So she was horny. This was exactly how men must feel when they had to have sex. She couldn't stop thinking about tearing off her clothes and then tearing off his clothes and then doing what they did best. She wasn't interested in discussing politics with Zach or taking in the sights of Atlanta or learning about his favorite books. No, she just wanted to get naked.

Kelly frowned. That wasn't exactly true. She did enjoy talking to him and she wouldn't mind getting to know him a little better. She glanced down at the phone, then reached for it. He was just seven numbers away. Closing her eyes, she took a deep breath then removed her hand from the phone.

What good would it do to start it all up again? She wasn't even sure she'd be staying in Atlanta. And if she decided to go back to L.A., it would be much more difficult to leave with him back in her life again. The temporary pleasures she might find in his body were far outweighed by the difficulty she'd have in letting him go a second time.

If all this indecision was what came with living in such close proximity to Zach Haas, then maybe staying in Atlanta wasn't such a good idea after all.

ZACH STOOD OUTSIDE Nicole's office, leaning against the wall and waiting for her to get off the phone. He wasn't exactly sure how he planned to get Kelly's number from Nicole, but he'd always been fast on his feet. He'd come up with a story if needed.

He heard her hang up the phone, then moved to stand

in the doorway. "Jeff finished editing the 'Younger Man' segments," he said. "You can check them out anytime."

Nicole nodded. "What did you think? Did you like them?"

"I'm kind of biased," Zach said with a grin.

"Jane says you're almost prettier than that actress we hired."

He cleared his throat. "Speaking of that actress, do you have any contact information for her? I have a buddy who's casting a commercial and I think she'd be great for one of the parts."

Nicole nodded, then shuffled through a pile of file folders on her desk. She found the one she was looking for, then grabbed a notepad and scribbled out a phone number. "I just have the number for her agent," she said, tearing the sheet off the pad and holding it out. "I'm sure she'll be able to get in touch with her."

"Thanks," Zach said, grabbing the paper and tucking it into his pants pocket.

"Was there something going on between you two?" Nicole asked as he turned to leave.

"Why?"

"I don't know. We were watching the footage and there just seemed to be something there."

He shook his head. "No. We were just acting."

"Are you sure? You were late for work two days in a row and you're never late."

"My alarm clock was broken," Zach lied. "It took me a while to get a new one."

"Right," Nicole said, nodding. "Well, when you talk to Kelly Castelle, tell her that we loved the stuff she did for us. The show's going to be taped next week and is scheduled to air the following week. We'll be sure to send her a dub."

"I'll tell her that," Zach said. He walked straight back to his cubicle then grabbed his cell phone and the phone number from his pants pocket. Flopping down in his office chair, he quickly dialed the number and waited as it rang.

Her agency picked up after two rings and Zach was surprised to be talking directly with Kelly's agent, Louise DiMarco. "I need to contact Kelly," he explained. "I was involved in her shoot for *Just Between Us* and I think she'd be perfect for a commercial we're shooting here in Atlanta. Can you get me her number?"

"Well, isn't that a stroke of luck," Louise said. "Kelly is still in Atlanta. She's supposed to call me this afternoon and check in. I can give her your number."

Zach drew a sharp breath. "She's still in Atlanta?"

"Yes," Louise replied.

He cleared his throat and tried to sound indifferent to the news. "Why don't you give me her number here and I'll contact her directly. Maybe I can get her a script before the end of the day." To Zach's relief, Louise didn't have any qualms about giving out Kelly's cell-phone number.

"And if you don't get an answer, I understand she's been working at a shop one of her friends owns. You could leave a message for her there. I think it's called Sweet Nothings. I have the number here somewhere."

"I know it," Zach said. "I'll try both numbers."

"And I'll wait to hear from you about any contract negotiations," Louise said.

"Thanks," he said. He snapped his phone shut and shoved it back into his pocket, then pulled a phone book from the shelf above his desk. "Sweet Nothings," he murmured. "Sweet Nothings." He found the address then grabbed a pen and wrote it on his palm.

He checked out on the callboard, and headed out the rear door of the studio to the parking lot. The shop was only a ten-minute drive from midtown, but traffic was always tricky around rush hour. By the time he reached Sweet Nothings it was nearly six. He found a parking spot a half block from the store, then hopped out of his truck.

The sign in the window said the shop was open until six. He stepped inside the air-conditioned interior and glanced around. Everywhere he looked were racks of sexy bras and panties in pretty colors. It was like a fantasyland for guys.

He walked over to glass display case and began to study the lingerie inside. A moment later, he heard footsteps on the hardwood floor.

"May I help you?"

Zach slowly turned around to face Kelly. He feigned surprise. "Kelly? What are you doing here?"

She didn't have to feign surprise. He could see it in her expression. He was the last person she expected to walk in the door of the shop. "I—I've been working here. Helping Angie out while she's getting her new store up and running. What are you doing here?"

"I'm looking for a gift," he said.

"You want to give someone lingerie?"

"Yes," Zach replied. "That's what you sell here, right?"

Kelly nodded, clearly uneasy with his presence. "I was just about to close. But if you come back tomorrow morning, Angie will be able to help you."

"Oh, I'm afraid I can't wait," Zach said. "I really need a gift for tonight. You can help me, can't you? It won't take long to pick something out."

"All right," Kelly said reluctantly. "Do you have a size?"

"She's about your size," Zach said. He strolled over to a rack and picked out a sexy red bra and panties. He pointed to the panties. "What are these called?"

"Boy shorts," she said. "They're cut high across the back."

"Oh, I like that," he said. He held out the hanger in front of her. "It's hard to imagine what it would look like on, though." He paused, then gave her a charming smile. "Would you mind trying it on for me?"

Kelly gasped. "What?"

"It's not like I haven't seen it all before," Zach said. "Or have you forgotten that I've seen you naked?"

"Are you serious? You want me to model this for you?"

"Sure." He plucked a few more hangers off the rack and handed them to her with a quick grin. "These, too."

Her eyebrow arched as she considered his request. She still hadn't realized that he was teasing. She probably thought he was buying the lingerie for another woman. "Humor me," he said with a smile.

He saw her gaze soften slightly as she realized his intent. But would she agree to play along? Or had their time apart dulled her desire for him?

"You don't think I'll do it, do you?"

"I can only hope," he said. "But then, if you're too uptight to—"

"I am not uptight," Kelly snapped, looking down her nose at him. "You forget, I'm an actress." She snatched the hangers from his hand, then walked over to the front door and locked it. "The fitting rooms are in the back," she said, throwing the garments over her shoulder as she strolled past him.

"Do I get to watch you change?"

"In your dreams," she muttered.

Kelly disappeared behind a fitting-room door and Zach sprawled out in a comfortable leather chair. He picked up a copy of a women's magazine and flipped through the pages, stopping to examine the sexy ads. "Try the red one on first," he called.

The door swung open and Kelly braced her hands on the doorjamb, dressed in the red lingerie set. Zach laced his hands behind his head and took in the sight of her. God, she was gorgeous. Thankfully, they were alone in the store so he didn't have to think about dead bunnies. His arousal could proceed without embarrassment.

"Turn around," he ordered.

She slowly turned and he smiled as his eyes drifted to her backside. The little "boy shorts" as she called them, were cut high to reveal the soft curves of her bottom. When she faced him again, he let his gaze linger on her breasts. "Nice," he murmured. "What do you think?"

"I don't know the woman you're buying them for," she said, a smile playing at her lips. "Some women think red is a bit...obvious."

"And what do you think?"

"I think you should consider other options," she said.

"I'd like to see the black, please," Zach said. She disappeared inside the fitting room. "This is a real stroke of luck that you're working at this store. I'm not sure I would have been able to choose on my own."

"I'm so glad I'm able to help," Kelly said, her voice laced with sarcasm.

"Why didn't you call me when you decided to stay?" he asked.

She opened the door again, this time dressed in a black bra and bikini panties. "I wasn't sure how long I was planning to be in Atlanta. I'm still not sure."

"But you're here now," he said. That's all Zach really cared about. "What do you think of the black?"

Kelly glanced down and shrugged. "It's pretty. Most men think black is sexy. I know you do. But I think most women prefer to wear pastels."

Zach slowly got to his feet. "Which do you prefer?" He slowly crossed the room to stand in front of her. His desire was obvious from the bulge in his cargo shorts and he made a mental note to start wearing underwear if he planned to spend any more time with Kelly.

"I like pastels," she murmured, staring at his chest.

Zach reached down and slid his finger beneath the strap of the bra, gently caressing her shoulder. "I suppose I should check out that option before I make my decision."

"You didn't choose any pastels," she said.

"Why don't you choose something for me?" He watched as she walked up to a rack of lingerie in pretty pinks and blues and greens. She chose a lavender set and went back into the fitting room. But this time, she didn't bother to close the door.

Zach swallowed a moan as she turned her back and slipped out of the bra. She put the lavender bra on, then slid the black panties down over her hips and stepped out of them. If he had any doubts about her intentions, they'd been completely erased. She wanted him as much as he wanted her.

When she'd pulled the thong on, she walked out of the dressing room and stood in front of him, a smug smile on her face. She met his eyes with a haughty expression. Now she was daring him to react, daring him to touch her. "Well?"

"You're right," Zach said, his voice cracking slightly. He slipped his hands around her waist. "The pastels are much better."

"Would you like me to gift wrap these?" She leaned into him until her breasts were pressed against his chest.

Zach cleared his throat. "No, I'll pay for them and you can wear them home."

"They're for me?" Kelly asked, her mouth pursed into a playful pout.

"Of course," Zach replied. "Whom else would I be buying underwear for?" He dropped a gentle kiss on her lips. "I'm glad you decided to stay for a while."

Kelly wrapped her arms around his neck. "I'm not sure this will be good for either one of us," she said, eyeing him dubiously. "Especially if you keep daring me to take my clothes off in public."

"How can it be bad?" Zach asked. "Especially when it feels so good?" He pulled her hips against his and kissed her, his mouth coming down firmly on hers. She softened in his arms, sinking into him as he took possession of her lips and her tongue.

Zach skimmed his hands over her body. He didn't care whether she stayed a day or a week or for the rest of her life. For now, she was here, with him. He couldn't ask for anything more. "Promise me something," he murmured.

"I don't think we should make any promises," Kelly said.

"This one is simple. Promise me you'll wear that when I see you the next time." He reached into his pocket and withdrew his wallet, then pulled out a credit card. "Here. Put it on my card. Then I have to go."

"Go? Where?"

"I have a meeting," Zach explained. "It might go late. You're still at the hotel?"

Kelly shook her head. "No. I'm staying at a condo that Angie's husband owns. It's not far from here."

"Should I come over after my meeting?"

She stepped back from him, a frown marring her pretty features. "How late will it go?"

"Not too late. And if you're asleep, I'll just have to wake you up." He ran his hand down her back, resting it on her right hip as he drew her closer. "I've spent a week without you. I don't think I want to go another night."

"Maybe we should just take this slowly," Kelly suggested. "Besides, Angie and I are doing inventory tomorrow and I have to be here at seven."

"All right. But can I call you later?"

She nodded. "Yes. Let me give you my cell-phone number."

"I have it," he said.

Zach watched as she got dressed, then walked with her to the front of the store. He fought the urge to pull her into his arms and kiss her. If he did that, then he'd never make it to his meeting. Kelly had an uncanny knack for making him late.

"You know, I think I will take the underwear with me," he said.

"What are you going to do with it?" she asked.

"Oh, I don't know. Carry it around in my pocket, put it under my pillow, maybe wear it."

Kelly laughed as she placed his purchase in a pretty bag and handed it to him. "Thank you for shopping at Sweet Nothings. Come back again soon."

He chuckled. "Oh, you can count on it. This is the only place I'd buy my ladies' underwear."

THE HEAT REFUSED to leave Atlanta and when Zach picked Kelly up for lunch the next day, she was hoping that they'd find a nice, air-conditioned restaurant that served a bottom-less glass of iced tea. Instead, Zach had decided on a picnic lunch beneath a large shade tree in Piedmont Park.

Kelly yawned as she watched a bee lazily buzz around a flower in a nearby garden. Though they hadn't spent last night together in the same bed, they'd spent most of the night on the phone, talking until the wee hours of the morning. Even separated by distance there was palpable electricity between them and the conversation often turned to sex.

Kelly had never indulged in phone sex, but last night Zach had convinced her to give it a try and it had resulted in two very powerful orgasms, one on each end of the line. They had both fallen asleep with the phones still connected and then spoken again when they woke up a few hours later.

Kelly shook her head. There were times when she felt positively naughty. Was there anything that Zach couldn't convince her to try? Or was the desire between them so powerful that it had stripped her of every last inhibition?

"Are you sleepy?" he asked, stretching out beside her on the blanket.

"It's the weather," she said.

"I think it's more than the weather," he countered.

She smiled, her eyes closed. "All right, maybe it is. It's just that everything seems so…close. I never notice the weather in L.A. Here, it's a living, breathing thing. It seeps into every pore of my skin until I feel like I'm wading through taffy just to move."

At the same time, it had made her slow down. She didn't rush to get from place to place. She walked at an easy pace, she learned to relax and be more patient. She thought about all those old movies that took place in the deep South, how passions always ran high when the temperature rose. *The Long, Hot Summer...Cat on a Hot Tin Roof...A Streetcar Named Desire.* Kelly wasn't sure if there was a physiological reason for it, but in this heat, she hadn't been able to stop thinking about sex—more specifically, sex with Zach.

Suddenly, something cold touched her lips. Zach ran an ice cube back and forth, water dripping onto her skin. "You do look a little parched," he said.

"Wilted," Kelly corrected.

The ice cube slipped over her chin and down along her throat until it came to rest in the notch of her collarbone. "How does that feel?"

"Nice," she said. He bent over her and licked the water from her skin, then continued to trace a path over her chest.

"I love the way you taste," he murmured, pressing his mouth against the top of her breast.

Kelly braced herself on her elbows and opened her eyes, longing for a cool breeze to rustle the tree above her head. She watched as he moved the ice cube to her bare shoulder, following the path with his tongue. "You'd better not start something you can't finish," she warned. "We both have to get back to work."

Zach sighed and tossed the ice cube into the grass. "Party pooper," he said.

Kelly giggled, then laid back down and closed her eyes. When she opened them again and glanced over at Zach, he had a small video camera trained on her face.

"What are you doing?"

"I'm taping you," he said.

"Don't," Kelly complained, holding up her hand.

"You're beautiful," Zach insisted. "Come on, you've been on camera before. You can see it, can't you?"

"See what?"

"How the camera loves you?"

"I know many Hollywood casting agents who would disagree with that assessment."

"Idiots, all of them," Zach muttered. He moved down to her breasts and lingered there for a long time.

"I'm not so sure," Kelly said, crossing her arms over her chest.

Zach looked at her over the top of the camera, his gaze meeting hers. "Tell me about that," he said. "Tell me what it's like. Why do you want to be a star?"

"I never wanted to be a star," Kelly explained. "I just wanted to make my living acting. I started in New York and everyone there told me to go to the west coast. They said I had a look that was more suited to television and movies."

"Why did you become an actress?"

She smiled. "Now, that's a complicated question, Dr. Freud."

"Try to answer it."

Kelly hesitated, trying to put her thoughts in order before speaking. "When I was a girl, my parents used to fight a lot. My father is Portuguese and my mother is Irish and they used to have at it on a daily basis. I'd hide in my room and close my eyes and pretend I was someone else. Some days, I'd be a famous ballerina and other days, I'd be the most notorious female pirate in history. I was an astronaut and a sorceress and a safari guide in Africa. While they were arguing, I'd carry on these long, detailed conversations with myself—in character, mind you—so I wouldn't have to listen to them."

"Are they still together? Your parents?"

Kelly nodded. "And still fighting. I guess that's what works for them. And I suppose I owe my acting career to their dysfunctional marriage. My father is retired. He was a surgeon in Connecticut. Now they live in Portugal on a small estate that his family left him."

"You don't see them much?"

"I visit once a year, they come to L.A. every now and then. But I seem to get along better with them when I'm not trying to deal with their drama."

"Are you a good actress?"

"I used to think so," Kelly said. "It's easy, when you're young, to have confidence in your talents. But over time, events—people—chip away at it. Now, I'm not sure if I was good or even mediocre. If I was, I'd have a career, don't you think? Maybe I'm just very good at hiding inside the roles I play. Pretending, the same way I pretended as a kid."

"Tell me about the time you first knew you wanted to be an actress."

Kelly stared off into the distance, watching a couple kids play with a Frisbee. "It was in eighth grade. I went to a fancy prep school and we did *Diary of Anne Frank* and I played Anne. And everyone said I was good. Nobody expected me to be good, but I surprised them all. And I remember, I was standing on stage, pretending to be this poor Jewish girl and I glanced out in the audience and my mother and father were sitting in the second row and they were watching me and they were holding hands. And I felt so wonderful up there on that stage, so powerful, as if the world were suddenly right again and I'd made it that way." She drew a deep breath. "But it hasn't felt the same for a very long time."

"Is that why you didn't go back?"

"I'm not sure why I'm still here," she replied. "L.A. is my home, but lately, I don't feel comfortable there."

"What do you think about the system in Hollywood that discards women once they reach the age of thirty?"

"When I was under thirty, I didn't ever think about it. But now that I'm over thirty, I guess I've just accepted the fact that my worth has diminished. It's no different than an athlete or a dancer or even a singer, getting older. It's part of the reality of the profession."

"Do you think you're beautiful?"

Kelly looked directly into the camera. "What kind of question is that?"

"A simple question."

She closed her eyes, surprised at how much she'd already revealed to him. With the camera between them, she'd thought nothing of answering his questions, and now that she had, she wasn't sure whether she ought to go on. "If I say yes, I sound conceited. And if I say no, then I sound like I'm falsely modest."

"Are you beautiful? Give me an honest answer."

"Most people say I am."

"I'm interested in what *you* say," Zach countered.

"Do you think I'm beautiful?"

"You know I do."

"Then I guess I am," she said with a smile. Maybe that's all it took, she mused. For just one man to believe, truly believe, that she was the most beautiful woman in the world. It didn't matter what all the casting agents and the directors and the producers thought. In Zach's eyes, she was the most beautiful woman in the world. Maybe that was enough.

Kelly held out her hand. "Now, you give me the camera."

He shook his head. "Nope. I'm through with being on that side of the lens. My one gig as an actor was enough for me."

"You weren't that bad."

"I did it for one reason and one reason only. To seduce you."

She giggled, then lay back on the blanket, staring up into the bower of leaves. "It worked."

He set the camera down beside him and leaned over her, kissing her until she moaned beneath him. "I guess it did," he teased.

Kelly rolled to her side and then threw her arms around his neck and pinned him beneath her. He wriggled as she stretched out on top of him, holding his hands above his head. "And why do you hide on the other side of the camera?"

"I like to watch people," he said. "When I was kid, I was kind of shy and really awkward."

"I don't believe that."

"It's true. I just really came in to my looks after I got to college. Through most of high school, I was only about five-six. And then, the summer after my junior year, I grew six inches. Girls started noticing me and I wasn't sure why. But I figured it out soon enough."

"And then you started to exploit it?"

"No. Enjoy it. But I never really felt comfortable with it. I liked being able to stand on the sidelines and watch people. I found an old camera of my dad's, a thirty-five millimeter, and I used to take it everywhere, snapping pictures, studying people through the lens. I never had any money for film and even if I did, it cost too much to develop the pictures. And that was a few years before digital cameras were really affordable. But the good photos, I kept in my memory. The first real photo I took was of my grandfather. He was just sitting on the porch of his house in Saratoga Springs, smoking his pipe and watching the world go by. I entered it in a student contest and won first prize. I used the money to buy a video camera and that's when I started to make movies. I could tape over and over on the same cassette and then watch what I taped. When I was in high school, I started editing my movies."

"Do you still make movies?"

"I'm making one now," he said, pointing to the camera.

"What's it about?"

"About a beautiful, sexy woman who drives me absolutely wild every time she touches me."

"Sounds like a porno," she said.

He shook his head. "It's an art film. Very tasteful. With a nude scene that's integral to the plot."

"People won't find it very interesting. There's no drama in my life. And I don't do nude scenes."

"There doesn't need to be drama," Zach explained. "Sometimes, ordinary life is worth examining more closely. Watching the conflicts we face, the decisions we make. There's beauty in the simplicity and the complexities of every day."

"All right," she said. "But if I'm starring in your home movie I want a share of the gross box office."

"I'll give you a share of the net," he said.

"Oh, no. Even I know that's a bad deal. And I want top billing. My name above the title. And I want an air-conditioned dressing room and a personal trainer and fresh flowers every day."

"Anything else?"

"Yes. I want you to make love to me, passionately and often, in fact, on demand."

"Now, those are terms I can live with," Zach said, chuckling. "But we're going to have to negotiate on the rest."

"All right. But I'll take a kiss now. Kind of like an advance on my shares."

He pulled her down and his lips met hers. He nibbled softly, then traced a line along her bottom lip with his tongue. When she opened her mouth, their tongues tangled and he moaned softly. "I like this," Zach murmured. "Usually the director never gets the girl. The handsome costar does."

She moved above him, his arousal hard between them. It didn't take much to get Zach going. Zach smoothed his hands over her back and them slipped them beneath her blouse. "What time do you get finished with work?" he asked.

"Angie is closing. I have to drop the deposit around 4:00 p.m., but that only takes a few minutes."

"Good. Then I'll pick you up at your place around five. I'm going to take you out tonight. On a date."

"I thought that's what this was."

"No, this was lunch. We both had to eat so we ate together. A date is different."

"I'm not sure I understand," Kelly said.

"I don't, either. But it sounded good when it was in my head. Just say yes."

"Yes," Kelly said. "I will go out on a date with you, Zach Haas."

She hadn't even considered saying no. As long as she was in Atlanta, she planned to spend as much time as possible with Zach. Why even try to resist her attraction to him? They had fun together and the sex was incredible and who knows if she'd ever feel this way with a man again. And after last night, she didn't want to spend another night without him in her bed.

For now, she'd allow herself this fantasy and deal with the consequences later.

5

ZACH OPENED HIS can of Dr Pepper as he walked back to his cubicle, the latest issue of *Sports Illustrated* tucked under his arm. Even after his nice, long lunch with Kelly he was already looking forward to their date that evening. As he rounded the corner, he saw Nicole bent over his desk, scribbling a note on his message pad.

"Looking for me?" he asked.

She glanced over her shoulder. "I was. Do you have my copy of the revised production schedule? I had it in the production meeting this morning and someone must have picked it up by mistake. I can't find it and it has all my notes on it."

Zach leafed through the stack of papers on his desk, then pulled out a sheaf marked with fluorescent green and Nicole's familiar scribble. "Sorry," he said.

"You had a message." She handed him the pink slip, then hitched her hands on her waist as she recited its contents. "Kelly called to say that she will meet you at the store at five instead of the condo." Nicole's eyebrow arched. "Is that Kelly as in Kelly Castelle?"

"Maybe," Zach said, regarding her suspiciously.

"Didn't we send her back to L.A.?"

"She has a friend here. She decided to stay for a while."
He took another sip of his pop, watching Nicole over the
rim of the can.

"And... Do you two have something going on?"

"Maybe," Zach repeated.

Nicole groaned. "Come on, Zach. I'm not nosy, I'm just
curious...for purely professional reasons."

"How does my personal life have anything to do with
your professional life?" Zach asked.

"You're a younger man. She's an older woman. You do
the math. If you've got something going, then maybe we
should invite Kelly to appear on the show next week. She's
bright, she's attractive and well-spoken, the perfect guest.
And I'd never have pegged her as the type to go for a
younger guy."

"Why not?" Zach asked.

"I don't know. She seems so...sensible. And self-aware.
Besides, it would be a great hook. You two met doing the skit
and now you're involved." Nicole gave him a penetrating
stare. "How involved are you? Have you two...you know..."

"I know? I know what?"

"Are you lovers?" Nicole whispered.

Zach leaned closer. "That's none of your business," he
whispered back. He sighed at her resigned expression.
"All right. We're going out on our first official date tonight.
I'm taking her to the Falcons game."

"I thought you were working at the Falcons game,"
Nicole said.

"I am. But I'm taking her along to watch and then later, we'll go out for a few drinks and maybe something to eat."

Nicole laughed. "That's your idea of an impressive first date? You're taking her to a football game so she can watch you work?"

"It's an NFL game."

She shook her head. "Zach, you poor thing. We've always wondered why you didn't have a girlfriend and now it's painfully clear. How much fun could this woman possibly have watching you stand behind a camera while you watch the game?"

"She's going to be sitting in an air-conditioned skybox with some guys I know," Zach said. "There'll be food and wine and comfortable chairs. It's not like I'm asking her to sit outside in zero-degree weather."

"It's a football game," Nicole said.

"Maybe she likes football. A lot of women do."

"And a lot of women say they do and they secretly hate it. Did you ask her? Did she tell you she liked football?"

"She doesn't know we're going to the game yet. I thought I'd surprise her."

"Oh, she'll be very surprised," Nicole said. She glanced at her watch. "You have a half hour before you have to pick her up." She grabbed his shirtsleeve and tugged him along with her. "Come on. Come with me. We'll do some pre-game damage control."

They walked through the hall to a small storage room known as the gift room. Sponsors and vendors often sent samples that were given away on the show as prizes or in audience goody bags. Nicole threw the door open and stepped inside. She grabbed a *Just Between Us* tote bag and handed it to Zach.

"All right," she said as she scanned the shelves. She held up a copy of *In Style* magazine, then put it into the bag. "We'll call this a football survival kit. Latest issue of *In Style*. Every woman loves *In Style*. Here—OPI nail polish. The best nail polish in the world. And here we have a few bestselling novels. Oh, and this is one of those little music players. I think it's already loaded with music."

"Thanks," Zach said. "But I really think she's going to want to watch the game."

"If she were twenty-one, she'd pretend to love the game and hang on every play and discuss it over margaritas afterward. If she were twenty-six, she might feign interest but be redecorating her apartment in her head while staring at the field. At thirty-one, she'd find a quiet corner in the stadium and read a magazine. At thirty-five, Kelly will find out where she's going and then ask if you'd mind if she stayed home instead and cleaned her oven."

Zach looked inside the tote bag and winced. "What else do you have?"

"Oh, this is really good," Nicole said, grabbing a gold box tied with a ribbon. "Godiva chocolates. Here, I'll put in two. And these pralines are from a candy maker in New Orleans. Very famous and absolutely delicious. And here's a nice sports watch so she can count down the minutes until she gets to go home. And I'll put in a bottle of this gourmet root beer, too." She stood back, her hands on her hips. "That should make up for your blunder. And in return for my saving your butt, I want you to ask Kelly Castelle if she'd be willing to appear on the show."

"I'll ask," Zach said, "but I don't think she'll agree."

"Fair enough. Now, you'd better get going. You don't want to be late."

Zach thanked Nicole again, then walked back to his cubicle and grabbed his car keys from his desk. But just as he was turning to go, his phone rang. He grabbed it, suspecting it might be Kelly, but it was Mindy at the reception desk.

"Zach, I have a guy on the phone. He says he's an attorney with the firm of Markson, DeWitt and Feld in New York City. He'd like to talk to you about a personal matter."

He'd never heard of the law firm, and as far as he knew, he'd paid all of his parking tickets before he'd left New York. "Did he say anything else?"

"He asked if I knew whether you had attended City University in New York before you moved to Atlanta. I said I thought you'd come from New York, but I wasn't sure you'd gone to school there."

Zach hesitated, his mind spinning with the possibilities. He'd left a lot of unfinished business behind in New York, but nothing that might make him the subject of a lawsuit. Unless… Oh, hell. He'd always been so careful to practice safe sex. What if some woman was claiming he was the father of her child?

He swallowed hard. "Take a message. No, wait. I'll talk to him."

"I'll put him through."

A moment later he heard the voice of Elliot Dunlop on the other end of the line. "Mr. Haas, I'm calling in regards to a lawsuit that's been filed against City University of New York and Dean Margaret Winters. I understand you've had some dealings with her."

"Am I being sued?" Zach asked.

"No. Actually, we're wondering if you might be a plaintiff to a lawsuit. Sexual harassment. It seems she's taken advantage of a number of male students, both before and after you."

Zach glanced at his watch. "I'm sorry, I really don't have time to talk. In fact, I've put this whole thing behind me. I'm cool with it. I'm dealing. And I really don't want to rock the boat, so I'm gonna have to say no on this one."

"But Mr. Haas, I think that coming forward would help all of the young men in—"

"Sorry." Zach quickly hung up the phone, then stared down at it, as if it had suddenly jumped up and bit him. He'd walked away from that time in his life, anxious to forget the mistakes he'd made and grateful that the scandal hadn't followed him here. The lottery would give him a chance to start all over again, to do what he'd always wanted to do. He didn't need a chance to relive all the stupid things he'd done to himself. Someone else could make Margaret Winters pay. It wouldn't be him.

Kelly was waiting for him when he arrived at Sweet Nothings. She changed into a pretty blue sundress that showed off her beautiful arms and shoulders and a colorful scarf tied through her dark hair. Zach sent a silent thank-you to Nicole. He wanted the evening to go well.

It was obvious they shared an incredible passion inside the bedroom. But Zach wanted more than that. He wanted a relationship outside, as well. There was more to Kelly than her body and he'd found himself caught up in discovering the woman she truly was. He replayed every conversation they had over and over again in his head, searching for clues about the depth of her feelings for him, about her intentions for the future.

Yet, the moment he was with her, the only thing he could think about was losing himself in the warmth of her body. Making love to her was proof that they belonged together, that they fit perfectly. There were moments in the midst of their passion that he felt as if he had touched her soul. He didn't want to spend a single minute apart from her.

"You look beautiful," he said, pulling her into his arms. His lips found hers and he kissed her, taking a deep lazy taste of her mouth. Zach's hands slid down her back to her bottom and he pulled her against him, already growing aroused by the feel of her in his arms. They had ten minutes. He could do a lot with ten minutes, he mused.

It was only natural to think about sex, but he needed to be careful. He wanted to prove to Kelly that they could enjoy much more together than just what they enjoyed in bed. He had a lot more to offer her than earth-shattering orgasms and a warm body to sleep next to. So he'd work on charming her outside the bedroom and seducing her inside the bedroom. That way, she'd never be able to resist him.

"Tell me the truth," he said, staring down into her pretty green eyes.

"About what?"

"I'm taking you to a Falcons game tonight."

"The bird?"

Zach groaned inwardly. "An NFL football team here in Atlanta? They're called the Falcons."

"Oh," Kelly said. "All right. Football."

He didn't hear a trace of interest or excitement in her voice. "And I know you might not get in to football, and that's all right, too. And if you'd rather stay home and clean your oven, I'll understand. Don't feel as if you have to go just because I asked you."

"I—I don't," Kelly said, frowning. "I've never been to a NFL game before and it might be interesting. And why would I want to clean my oven? I've never cleaned an oven in my life."

Zach chuckled softly, then grabbed her hand and walked with her out to the street where he'd double-parked the truck. He helped her inside, then circled around and got in behind the wheel. But before he pulled out into traffic, he handed her the tote bag. "In case you get bored with the game. It's kind of like a football survival kit."

She pulled out the nail polish. "Oh, I love this stuff. And Godiva chocolates? Oh, *In Style!* My favorite magazine." Kelly leaned over and kissed him, her lips warm on his cheek. "Thanks. This will really be fun. Fashion and football. What more could a girl want?"

As they drove to the stadium, Zach took every opportunity to watch Kelly and to touch her. He grabbed her hand and pulled it to his mouth, gently kissing her fingertips. Though they hadn't spoken about spending the night together, Zach knew it was inevitable. He could feel the tension pulsing between them and there was nothing to do about it except to find release later on in each other's arms.

The age difference, which at first had seemed like such a big deal, had become a nonissue. When they were together, they were just two people, wildly attracted to each other. And though the attraction had been purely physical at first, things were changing between them.

He'd never been in love. Hell, he wasn't sure he'd recognize love if it kicked him in the ass. In the past, he'd become involved with older women because he hadn't had to consider love. They'd always been satisfied with a sexual relationship only. But this time around, with Kelly, maybe he wouldn't be satisfied with that. Maybe he'd want more.

Zach fixed his gaze on the street ahead. He'd be a fool to fall in love with her. Tomorrow she could decide to go back to L.A. and then where would that leave him? Besides, he was too smart to get himself in to that kind of mess again. He didn't need to love women in order to…well, love them.

When they reached the Georgia Dome, Zach steered the truck into a parking area for ESPN employees. He grabbed Kelly's hand as they walked inside through a special entrance, flashing his pass at the security guard. Now that he was here, Zach wondered if maybe he had made a mistake. How much fun was she going to have sitting all alone with a bunch of strangers?

Zach pulled her to a stop. "Here's the thing. I have to work this game. I'm a freelance cameraman for the network. So we won't be sitting together. You'll be in one of the luxury boxes with a buddy of mine. His wife will be there, too. And I'll be across the stadium. But as soon as the game is over, we'll go out and get a drink, maybe get something to eat?" He paused. "You're not angry at me, are you?"

Kelly frowned. "Angry? Why would I be angry?"

"Well, I'm kinda deserting you."

"Zach, I'm perfectly capable of taking care of myself. I do a lot of things alone. I go to the movies alone, I go out to dinner alone. I'm not afraid to be left alone for a few hours."

Zach stared down into her face, his hand smoothing over her cheek to tangle in her hair. He gently pushed her back into the shadows and kissed her. "You're incredible," he murmured against her damp lips.

"You should probably get going," Kelly said. "You're going to be late."

Zach reached in his pocket and pulled out the pass for the skybox. "Here. Go up this ramp and show this to any one of the ushers and they'll be able to get you to where you're going. Introduce yourself to Mike and Jeannie and have a good time. I'll come up after the game and get you, so wait up there." He grabbed another quick kiss. "I'll see you in a little bit."

He left her standing beside a pillar, a shaft of light streaming down on her. Kelly gave him a wave then blew him a kiss and Zach laughed. How the hell did he ever get this lucky? He'd always enjoyed women, their looks, their smell, their bodies. But he'd never really wanted much more than that.

With Kelly, he wanted to learn everything there was to know about her—her favorite color, her first kiss, how she really felt about him. He wanted to look at her and know, deep in his heart, she belonged to him and no one else.

But could she forget the eleven years that stood between them and see him for what he was, a man completely captivated by her beauty? Or would he always be the younger man, entertaining in bed, but nothing more?

Zach was determined to answer those questions, but he wasn't sure he'd be happy with the answers he found.

KELLY FOUND THE skybox without a hitch and she was surprised to find a group of men already in the midst of a party. Mike, Zach's friend, immediately apologized for his wife's absence, then gave her a ten-cent tour of the skybox.

The room was comfortably furnished with sofas and chairs, some of which were turned to the wall of glass that overlooked the playing field. There was a bar and a television monitor and a buffet loaded with an array of food. There was even a private bathroom. A door led to the outside seating.

Mike grabbed a bottle of champagne from the refrigerator beneath the bar and poured her a glass, then introduced her to the rest of the guests, seven men, all well-dressed and successful and all about her age or a bit older.

This was where all the good men were, Kelly mused. The real gentlemen, with real jobs. Not the plastic men who inhabited Hollywood, but men who were funny and charming and polite. Though she was the only woman present, she felt completely comfortable, and before long, Kelly had a crowd gathered around her as she told Hollywood stories.

By the time the game started, the champagne had gone to her head and she was laughing at the bawdy jokes and flirting with all the men, single and married. They brought her food and more champagne and patiently explained the game to her. And they gave her a Falcons cap to wear.

Then, before she even realized that three hours had passed, the game was nearly over. She walked out the door to the stadium seats and sat down in the first row, bracing her arms on the rail. The stadium was packed with people and it was impossible to see where the cameras were located.

"I think he's over there somewhere next to the scoreboard," Mike said, sitting next to her.

Kelly followed his direction to the center tier just above the end zone. A time-out was called on the field and music filled the stadium. A moment later a cheer went up and Mike pointed to the huge television screen. "Look, there you are!"

Kelly stared at the screen and then laughed. Obviously, Zach had found her. She smiled and waved, then blew him a kiss. That only brought a bigger cheer from the crowd and she gave the camera a coy look and blew another kiss. A second later, her face was replaced by video of a pickup truck going up the side of a mountain.

"They can tell a movie star when they see one," Mike teased.

"I'm not a star," Kelly said. "Far from it. In fact, right now, I work in a lingerie store."

"Maybe this was your big break, kind of like when they found Marilyn Monroe in that drug store."

"Schwab's," Kelly said. "And that was Lana Turner. Marilyn Monroe was discovered next to the swimming pool at her apartment building."

"From Schwab's to the JumboTron at the Georgia Dome. You never know."

Kelly didn't have the heart to tell him that her days of being discovered were long over. They'd all just assumed she was younger, since she was Zach's date, and she hadn't bothered to correct them. It felt good to be looked at in a different way. And they all seemed so impressed when she listed her credits. They might not have been so dazzled if they knew that it was the sum total of nearly fifteen years in L.A.

The game clock wound down and before long, Mike and the rest of the boys were ready to head home. He offered to stay with Kelly until Zach arrived, but she assured him she'd be fine on her own.

She curled up on the sofa with her copy of *In Style* and flipped through it. But the champagne had made her drowsy and before she knew it, she'd dozed off. When she woke, she found Zach sitting across from her in an easy chair, his gaze fixed on her face, a drink in his hand.

Kelly pushed up on her elbow and brushed her hair out of her eyes. "Hi," she breathed. "When did you get here?"

He shrugged. "I don't know. Ten, fifteen minutes ago."

"Are you finished?"

He nodded. "It looks like you've had a good time." He nodded to the empty champagne bottle on the coffee table.

His tone was flat and his expression cold. Kelly knew right away that he was upset about something. "I had a very nice time. Mike and his friends made the game a lot of fun."

He nodded. "I bet they did."

There it was. She could hear it in his voice, in the sarcastic edge to his words. There were moments when she forgot his age, forgot that he was only twenty-four, but this wasn't one of them. Zach was jealous, angry that she'd managed to have such a good time without him, and he was taking it out on her. She'd spent the evening with a group of handsome, successful men and he felt insecure. "I would have much rather spent the evening alone with you."

"I shouldn't have brought you here. I should have taken you on a real date. Nicole was right."

"Nicole? From the station?"

"She's the one who said you wouldn't be interested in football. I just didn't expect you to be interested in the rest of the guys watching football."

"You were watching me through the camera?" she asked.

"Every time I looked over here, you were deep in conversation with a different guy."

"I was just being friendly. And maybe I was flirting a little. But it didn't mean anything. There's nothing to be jealous of." She'd never imagined that Zach could be insecure about anything, especially from where he stood in comparison to other men! He was handsome and smart and charming, the kind of guy who could walk into a room and have every woman drooling over him within minutes, and every guy wanting to be his best friend. The fact that he didn't possess even an ounce of narcissism made him even more attractive.

"I'm not jealous," he snapped. "It's just that—sometimes I wonder if there's anything that you could possibly find interesting about me."

Kelly crawled off the sofa and crossed to his chair, then sat down on his lap, determined to soothe his fears. "I wonder the same thing—what you find so fascinating about me."

"All the guys on the crew were talking about you," he said. "They were calling you the girl with the lips." He reached up and brushed a lock of hair from her cheek. "You looked beautiful. The camera loves you."

He wove his fingers through the hair at her nape and pulled her down until her mouth met his. It was so easy to forget the years between them when he kissed her. But his insecurities just brought them all back. He was still naive enough to believe that every guy in the world was interested in her, just because he was. The notion was as far from reality as an idea could get. She hadn't had a steady boyfriend in almost three years.

"Most of the guys in the Georgia Dome loved you." He kissed her again. "And I love you," he murmured, his breath warm against her lips.

Kelly knew he didn't mean *love* in the serious sense of the word. It was so simple for Zach to toss the word out there. He didn't know how complicated love could be, how it was dangerous to say it, even when the sentiment might be real. She curled into his lap and lost herself in the heat of his kiss.

His fingers moved to the bodice of her dress and he slowly worked at the tiny buttons until he'd exposed the lacy bra beneath. Kelly glanced over at the door, knowing it was unlocked. But she didn't care. When he pulled aside the fabric and drew her nipple into his mouth, a shiver coursed through her body. Making love to Zach always seemed a tiny bit dangerous.

She sighed, closing her eyes and enjoying the flood of sensation that washed over her body. He had a way of touching her that was so exquisitely intense, as if every ounce of his being was focused on pleasuring her. His lips trailed over her skin, leaving a damp imprint along the way.

Zach grabbed her waist and pulled her up until she straddled him in the chair, her knees at his hips. His fingers tangled in the straps of her sundress, then gradually worked the bodice down until it hung around her waist. Reaching back, Kelly undid her bra and let it fall off her shoulders. He tossed it aside, then drew her to him, fixing his mouth on her breast again.

No matter how much she wanted to resist him, Kelly had learned that it was useless. The moment Zach touched her, she wanted more. He satisfied a longing she never knew she had, a need so deeply hidden that only he had been able to reveal it.

She wanted to be seduced, to be overwhelmed with desire. When he touched her it was pure lust, a man wanting nothing more than her body to satisfy his need. It was simple, elemental, this raw passion that they seemed to share. And with every moment they spent together, she felt more desperate to indulge.

Kelly grabbed the hem of his shirt and pulled it up over his head, then tossed it aside. She smoothed her palms over his chest, then slid off the chair to kneel in front of him. Teasing at his nipples with her tongue, Kelly unbuttoned his jeans.

He watched as she worked at his zipper, then stretched his legs out on either side of her. He needed reassurance, needed to know that he was the only man she desired. She grabbed the waistband of his pants and tugged them down, exposing his rigid shaft.

He was beautiful, Kelly mused, wrapping her fingers around him. His body was achingly perfect in every way and she took pleasure in just looking at him—and even more pleasure in touching him. She slowly began to stroke and Zach moaned softly, tipping his head back to rest on the chair.

He'd once seduced her with his mouth and now, she wanted to do the same, to bring him to the edge and beyond with her lips and tongue. Kelly began slowly, teasing him at first, making him groan in frustration. He kept his hands above his head, as if he were determined not to interfere with anything she did, but rather would enjoy it as it was offered.

She brought him close, over and over, and each time, his breathing grew more ragged. He whispered her name, urging her on, and Kelly felt powerful, as if she had touched on the part of him that was most vulnerable. But in the end, he took control away.

Zach stood, his jeans falling low on his hips. He pulled her along to the sofa, then pushed her down until she lay stretched out on the soft suede. Slipping his hands beneath her skirt, he slowly pushed the fabric up along her legs.

She knew how it would feel and as he pulled her panties down, she tried to prepare herself. But the shock of his tongue on her sex still took her breath away. He knew exactly how to make her ache, how to bring her to the edge and then just stop short. It was as if he were repaying her for what she'd done to him, showing her that he could make her beg for release in the same way he had.

Kelly lost herself in the delicious game, her desire spinning out of control, then slowing for a time, leaving her dizzy. When she become lucid enough to think rationally, she ran her fingers through his hair and slowly drew him away. "Do you have a condom?" she whispered.

He nodded, reaching into the back pocket of his jeans

to pull one out of his wallet. She snatched it from his fingers and tore the package open, then with trembling hands smoothed it over his shaft. She lay back on the sofa and pulled him along with her.

A moment later, he was inside her, his arms braced on either side of her body. He slowly buried himself in her warmth, filling her completely then waiting until she moved beneath him. She'd never felt anything quite so perfect. Every time he entered her it was a revelation, proof that heaven did exist.

Though they were still partially dressed, there was enough exposed flesh to touch and kiss. Kelly ran her hands from his shoulders to the small of his back and then lower. He was all smooth skin and lean muscle and when he began to move inside her, the muscles tensed and shifted beneath her palms.

He began slowly and Kelly matched his movements with her own, arching against him with each thrust until he was deep inside of her. This only seemed to spur him on and he increased his tempo. Kelly buried her face against his arm, biting at the hard muscle of his biceps and inhaling the scent of his skin.

She tried to take it all in, to absorb and enjoy each sensation, but the pleasure began to muddle her mind and in the end, Kelly couldn't separate her reaction from the man moving above. Every movement seemed to bring another more intense sensation until they came, one after the other, like waves on a beach.

Her orgasm took her by complete surprise and she dissolved into spasms that rocked her entire body. She opened her eyes and watched as his release grew close, the focused expression set on his handsome face, his lip caught between his teeth.

She pressed her forehead against his as he drove into her. And then, he moaned and gasped, surrendering to the desire. All the rest of the world seemed to fall away at that moment and Kelly felt as if they were the only two people left on the planet, the only two who populated this world they'd made for themselves.

What they had between them was perfect. And they were the only ones who could spoil it. The prospect of staying in Atlanta, with Zach, was growing more tempting with every hour that passed. Though she didn't want to make a decision about her life so quickly, Kelly was beginning to believe the choice had already been made.

It had been made the very first time she touched him.

ZACH CURLED UP against the warm body next to him, throwing his leg over hers and drawing her closer. Early morning light streamed through the windows of Kelly's bedroom. He smiled to himself. It was nice to wake up with her again, to have his very first sight in the morning be her dark hair or her beautiful face—or her naked body.

He smoothed his hand along her hip, her soft skin warm beneath his palm. She stirred, then slowly rolled over to face him. "What time is it?"

"Early," he said.

"I have to open the shop at ten," she murmured, nuzzling into his chest.

"You have time." Zach pressed a kiss to her forehead. "I'm going to go get us some breakfast. How do you take your coffee?" It was a simple question and when she replied in great detail, he was pleased. It was just one small thing to know about her—sixteen-ounce skim latte, no foam, with two sugars.

"Anything to eat?" he asked.

"The most I can take in the morning is toast or a bagel." She rolled over on her stomach. "I'm going to get in the shower."

Zach crawled on top of her and kissed the spot beneath the nape of her neck. "Not yet," he said. "Wait until after breakfast. Then I'll join you."

"Don't you have to work?"

"Larry is covering for me today so I'm just helping out in editing. And Jeff never rolls in till noon, so we can have a lazy morning."

"Latte, please," she murmured, burying her face in the pillow.

Zach hopped out of bed and searched for his pants, finding them at the foot of the bed. He tugged them on, then grabbed his shirt and pulled it over his head. He'd kicked off his shoes at the door and slipped them on before he began a search for Kelly's keys. Once he'd found them, he headed out.

Her condo was in a busy part of midtown, with three or four coffee shops within a one-mile radius. He picked a small shop that he visited often, parking his truck in a loading zone while he ran inside. After placing his order, he walked back out to the sidewalk and bought a newspaper from a nearby box.

He flipped open the front page and scanned for the weather report. "High of ninety-six, chance of storms in the afternoon," he mused.

A photo in the lower right-hand corner of the page caught his attention and Zach gasped. There was a small article about the Falcons' victory the night before and right above it was an image of Kelly, wearing a Falcons' cap and blowing a kiss at the camera. The photo had an ESPN credit and Zach was certain it was a capture from the video feed off his camera.

"'Fans love the Falcons,'" he read from the headline. "'The Falcons snatched a preseason victory from the Chicago Bears last night, the team spurred on by a lucky kiss from an unknown female fan. Details in sports.'"

He chuckled to himself. Good to know that he wasn't the only one who thought the camera loved Kelly. He wondered if she ever took a bad photo. Most people weren't photogenic from all angles, but she was. God, she looked so sexy, her lips puckered in a perfect kiss, her eyes bright with humor.

When he got back to the condo, he grabbed the newspaper and tucked it under his arm, balancing the coffees in one hand as he jumped out of the truck. Kelly was exactly where he'd left her, snuggled beneath the down comforter, the air conditioner keeping the condo at a pleasant temperature.

Zach set the coffees down on the bedside table and sat on the edge of the bed. "Are you awake?"

"Ummm," she replied.

"There's something interesting in the paper," he said. "I think you should see it."

Kelly opened one eye. "How is it you're so full of energy and I feel like I've been run over by a truck?"

"You drank a bottle of champagne last night," he said.

"Right," she murmured. She braced her hands beneath her then pushed up to a sitting position, the comforter falling away from her naked breasts. "So, what's in the paper? Please tell me they're expecting snow today in Atlanta."

Zach smiled to himself, wondering if he'd ever grow accustomed to seeing her naked, if it would ever cease to pique his desire. "You are in the paper," he said, holding out the front page.

Kelly rubbed her eyes, then stared down at her photo. "I look weird," she muttered. "I hate myself in hats. It makes me look like I've got a really tiny head."

"You look gorgeous," Zach countered.

The sound of a ringing cell phone split the silence and Zach looked around to find his phone on the floor beside the bed. He snatched it up and glanced at the caller ID, then flipped it open.

"Hello?"

"Zach Haas?"

"Yes?"

"This is Matt Orford. I was the assistant director at last night's game. I'm hoping you might be able to help me. The ESPN Web site and our main switchboard have been swamped with inquiries about the girl, the one you picked out of the crowd at the game last night. The girl with the lips. One of the cameramen thought you might have known her."

"I do," Zach said, glancing over at Kelly, who had pulled a pillow up over her head.

"I guess she's caused some big stir with the photo that appeared in the paper this morning. Some of the players have mentioned her in interviews and we've got some of the local news outlets interested in talking to her. Can you get me her phone number?"

"Can I get back to you on that, Matt?" Zach asked. "She's a bit difficult to reach and I want to clear this with her first. But I'll call you later this morning."

"The sooner the better. I wanted to pass this off to media relations but they won't take it until I have a contact name and number."

"I'll call you later," Zach said. He closed the phone and tucked it in his pocket. Though he found it amusing that one photo could cause such an uproar, Zach also knew the trouble that press scrutiny could cause. When he and the lottery group appeared at their first press conference, he'd thought he'd answer a few questions and then leave. But the questions became personal and reporters began to probe in the backgrounds of all the winners, hoping to find a juicy story there.

Details of their private lives leaked out and were discussed on news shows. Calls from investment managers and bankers and charities quickly followed, along with contacts from every crazy person in Georgia, looking for a quick handout. If Kelly's identity was revealed, then who knew what kind of nutcases would start following her around?

Zach reached out and peeked beneath the pillow. But then, she lived in Hollywood, she'd spent her life there trying to be noticed. Maybe if she got noticed in Atlanta, she'd have a reason to stick around for a while. "Are you going to lie in bed all morning?"

"Yes," she said.

"You don't want your coffee?"

"Yes." She sat up, tossing the pillow aside. "I do."

Zach handed it to her, then put the newspaper on her lap. "That call was from ESPN. They've been flooded with requests to know who you are and where you come from. It seems your little appearance on the JumboTron and on the network feed has caused some pretty intense interest."

"Really? Why?"

"Because you're gorgeous. What are you going to do about it?"

"I don't know." She stared at the photo for a long moment and shook her head. "A few weeks ago, I would have killed for this kind of publicity. But, now, it's too late."

Zach frowned. He thought she'd be excited or even annoyed. But he was totally unprepared for no reaction at all. "For what?"

"To make a difference." She groaned, then flopped back on the pillow, throwing her arm over her eyes and resting her coffee on her chest. "Why now? After all these years, why would it all start happening now?"

"If people are interested in you, then that should be a good thing, shouldn't it? Maybe you were just in the wrong city."

She drew a ragged breath and ran her fingers through her hair. "I've been thinking about leaving L.A. Or at least, leaving show business. Sooner or later, I'm going to have to face the fact that I can't make a living at acting. With every year that passes, I'm less and less employable." She glanced over at him. "You know that's true, don't you?"

"But you're a good actress," Zach said. He'd watched a lot of actresses in films and on television and his instincts were good. He forced a smile. But had his overwhelming desire for Kelly clouded his judgment? Did he see her talents through a passion-tinged prism?

"You've never really seen me act," she said.

"Yes, I have," Zach said. "A little."

Kelly reached out and touched his cheek with her palm. "Someday you'll make someone a really sweet boyfriend."

Zach frowned, then stood up, suddenly irritated by her condescending tone. "What is that supposed to mean?" He walked to the door of the bedroom, then turned around and returned to the bed. "I don't know why you can't believe there might be something between us. Why you automatically think that this is just a short-term thing."

"I—I don't," Kelly said, sitting up and setting her coffee aside.

"Yes, you do! If I were thirty or even twenty-seven, then you wouldn't have any qualms. You'd be thinking about how happy we could be, how we could have a future together. You'd be thinking about weddings and children and happily-ever-afters in some suburban house with a white picket fence."

"I would not," Kelly said.

"You know, all I really want is a fair shot here. A chance to prove that I'm not just some love-struck kid who doesn't know what he's doing. I want you. There, I've said it. I want you."

She opened her mouth, then snapped it shut again. "I don't want to fight," she finally said. "Why can't this just be what it is? Fun. Nothing serious. You don't want to—"

"Don't tell me what I want," Zach interrupted. Cursing beneath his breath, he grabbed her arm and pulled her to her knees, then kissed her. It wasn't a sweet, romantic kiss, but a deep, punishing kiss meant to prove his words. When he'd finished, he released her and she sank down on the bed, her eyes wide, her lips damp, her breath coming in short gasps.

"What do *you* want?" he demanded.

"I want to be ten years younger," she whispered with a rueful smile. "I want to forget everything I know about love. I want to forget about every man who's walked in and out of my life and hurt me or betrayed me or made me feel like a fool."

"Then do it," Zach said. "Forget about the past."

"That's easy to say when you don't have a past," she said.

"I don't think you want to know about my history with women," Zach said.

"You're right," Kelly said. "I haven't been fair to you.

What's happened in the past shouldn't make a difference between us." She drew a deep breath and looked into his eyes. "I'm sorry."

Zach sighed, then cupped her face in his hands and kissed her. "I'm sorry, too." He wiped an errant tear from her cheek and smiled. "See, that wasn't so bad. We had our first fight and we managed to get through it."

Kelly nodded.

He stood up beside the bed and took off his shirt, then slid out of his pants. A tiny smile quirked at the corners of her mouth as she watched him undress. Then she lifted the covers of the bed and crawled back beneath the comforter, holding it up so that he could join her.

When they were settled, Zach gathered her in his arms and kissed her again, taking his time to linger over her mouth, tracing the shape of it with his tongue.

It wouldn't do to look too far into the future with Kelly. He'd have to be happy to take just one day at a time and see where it went. But it was growing more difficult every day to imagine a life without her.

6

ANGIE STROLLED INTO the shop a few minutes before noon, dressed in faded jeans and a pale pink T-shirt. She wore a baseball cap on her head and her hair was pulled back into a ponytail.

"Morning," Kelly called from a spot behind the counter.

"I knew I'd seen him before!" Angie walked up to the counter and slapped a piece of paper down in front of Kelly. She smiled smugly. "Go ahead. Check it out."

"Check what out?"

"Zach Haas. From the moment I met him, it's bothered me. I knew him from somewhere and I just couldn't place him. So last night, I was Googling for a Rocky Road brownie recipe and I typed in his name and there he was. Zach Haas."

"What? Is he some kind of ax murderer?"

"He's a millionaire," Angie said. "He and some of the employees at *Just Between Us* hit the Lot'o'Bucks lottery in April. They split thirty-five million dollars. Seven million each!"

"Zach? That can't be right. I mean, he would have said something."

"Maybe not," Angie said. "You know how some women are. They see a bank account and all of a sudden they're planning the wedding and talking about children."

Kelly scanned the article, pulled from the Internet site for the *Atlanta Journal-Constitution*. It listed some names she recognized: Eve Best, Nicole Reavis and Jane Kurtz. And she'd spoken to Cole Crawford on the phone about her contract. They'd all had a share in the lottery winning.

"I'm surprised he didn't tell me," she muttered. "It does seem a pretty important detail about his life to keep a secret."

"So, have you actual gotten to the details stage yet? Past lovers, secret fetishes, the way he takes his eggs?" Angie asked.

She thought about the day in the park, when he'd videotaped her and asked her all those personal questions. She'd revealed details of her life, but he hadn't said much about himself. Only that she wouldn't be interested in hearing about the women in his past.

"This morning we agreed we weren't going to talk about the past. That we were just going to concentrate on the present. But if he's presently a millionaire, it might be nice to know."

"Interesting. Maybe you should just ask him."

"How am I supposed to do that?"

Angie shrugged, then grabbed her bag and set it on the counter. "I'm sure there's a way to get him to tell you." She withdrew a copy of the morning paper and stared at the weather forecast, printed on the front page. "Hmm. A high of ninety-six today. I don't know why it is, but women don't buy sexy underwear when it's hot outside. You'd think they'd spend their evenings inside, walking around in their underwear, and they'd want to look nice."

"It's hard to feel pretty when your clothes are sticking to your skin and your hair is limp or frizzy."

"I guess you're right," Angie said. She flipped the paper over, then frowned. "Wow, look at this picture. This woman looks just like you. Gosh, she could be your twin sister."

"That is me," Kelly said. "It was taken last night at the football game."

"You're the girl with the lips?" Angie asked. "They were talking about it on the radio this morning, about how all the men at the game just went wild when your picture came up on the scoreboard. And then, I guess one of the TV commentators said he'd fallen in love with you and wanted to marry you. And that turned in to a big joke and now everyone is wondering who you are."

"Zach put me on TV and I blew a kiss to him. It was just a silly thing. People will forget about it. Don't worry."

"I don't think so," Angie said. "Don't you think you should take advantage of your fifteen seconds of fame? Don't you think everyone in Atlanta would love to know that you work at Sweet Nothings in Buckhead with a new location opening soon in midtown?"

Kelly laughed. "I guess publicity for the shop might be nice. But I don't want any stalkers coming in and bothering me. I think it's just best to let it all blow over."

"The radio station is offering a reward to the person who calls in and gives them your name."

"No one in Atlanta knows me, except for you and the people at *Just Between Us*."

"This could be really good for your career," Angie said.

"That's what Zach said. But it only makes things more complicated. I'm not sure I want that anymore. Maybe I'd be happy working here, living in Atlanta and…getting on with my life."

"Your life with Zach?"

Kelly shook her head. "I don't know. Everything is just so confusing." She groaned. "My life is…out of control. From the moment I stepped off that plane, I haven't been myself. And it seems to be getting worse." She pointed to the picture in the paper. "That's not me."

Angie reached into her purse and pulled out a pair of Gucci sunglasses. "Then you better wear these. And put your hair up under a hat. At least until everyone forgets this picture."

"Maybe I should just go back to L.A. where no one knows me."

Angie gave her a pleading look. "Don't. I love having you here. Why don't you just wait until your agent calls you with another job and then you can decide to stay or go. It's not worth going back if there's nothing there for you to do."

"I guess you're right."

"And besides, you wouldn't want to leave Zach, would you?"

Kelly groaned in frustration. "That's just it. The longer I stay, the more intense things get with him. I can't let myself fall for him. I just can't."

Angie paged through the paper. "Is he mean to you? Does he ignore you? Is the sex bad? Does he make you wait on him hand and foot?"

"Of course not. He's sweet and considerate and he waits on me. And the sex is incredible."

"Then hang on to him, honey, because men like that are few and far between. And if you don't snatch him up, somebody else will."

"But do you really think we could make a relationship work? I'm eleven years older than he is."

"Are you worried about how you feel or about what everyone else is going to say?"

Kelly had never thought of it that way. But Angie was right. She had no doubt that she could fall in love with Zach, if she gave herself the chance. She was afraid of what everyone would say if she did. But who was "everyone"? The only people who really counted in her life would be thrilled if she found a man to love. And she didn't care what strangers thought.

She threw her arms around Angie's neck and gave her a hug. "Thank you. I'm not sure I could have sorted this all out without you to talk to. It's nice to have a best friend again."

Angie smiled. "I know. I feel the same way."

"I have to go. Is that all right? I have to see Zach."

"Oh, take the afternoon off," she said, waving her hand.

"I have plenty to do here and if I go over to the new store, I'll just get in the way of the contractors."

"Thank you. I'll come back before six and help you close."

The bell for the front door sounded and Angie grinned. "He must have read your mind. See, you're already completely in sync with each other. It's a sign."

Kelly grabbed her purse from beneath the register and walked over to the door to greet Zach. "Hi. I was just going to come and see you."

"And I was coming to see you," he said. "Hey, Angie. How's business?"

"Slow," she called out. "I saw that you made a purchase the other night. Would you like to buy something else? We have some darling bustiers in your size."

Zach chuckled. "I'll come back later."

"Do you want to grab some lunch?" Kelly asked.

Zach nodded and placed his hand at the small of her back as they walked to the door. When they got to the truck, he paused before he turned on the ignition. "I have some bad news," he said. "One of the radio stations was offering a reward for your name and address and someone at the studio called it in. I'm not sure who it was since the radio station won't say, but they've already called Eve and questioned her about you. It's only a matter of time before they find you, Kelly. Maybe you ought to just talk to the press and get it over with."

"Can we go somewhere? Someplace quiet?" She swallowed. "I don't want to have to think about this right now."

"We can go to my place," Zach said.

She nodded, then stared out the passenger-side window as Zach pulled out into traffic. Kelly wasn't sure how she ought to take all this. A month ago, she might have been excited, hopeful, optimistic even. A person never knew where their big break might come from. But she already felt as if she'd left that part of her life behind.

If her Hollywood career were suddenly revived, would she want to go back? She liked working at Sweet Nothings and living a normal life. And she was growing more attached to Zach with every passing day. But she knew the lure of fame and its monetary compensation would be difficult to resist. She could make more with one small part in a movie than she could make all year at Sweet Nothings.

If her past romantic relationships had proven anything, she knew that she was the only one she could truly count on. Though she'd had serious relationships in the past, Kelly had always found herself with unavailable men, men who weren't ready to make an emotional commitment. So, it had always fallen to her own means to pay the bills and provide for herself, rather than trust any man to provide for her—even a man who had recently won millions of dollars.

She glanced over at Zach. Maybe that's why she'd jumped in to a relationship with Zach, because she'd assumed there would never be anything deeper between them beyond passionate sex. Besides, he didn't owe her an explanation about the money and she shouldn't need one.

After a fifteen-minute ride, they arrived in an industrial

section of town, redbrick warehouses built against narrow sidewalks. Zach pulled the truck up to the curb, then helped her out. They climbed a small flight of stairs and he unlocked a steel door.

"You live here?"

"It's not as luxurious as your condo. A friend of mine owns it. He uses it as studio space. He's a filmmaker and he's out of town a lot. I keep an eye on things and he gives me a break on the rent." He chuckled. "A hundred percent off."

Zach led her down a long hall to another steel door, then unlocked it and pulled it aside. She walked into a huge room, the space broken only by floor-to-ceiling brick pillars. Lighting equipment was scattered all around and one corner held shelves of sound equipment. The living area was on the far end of the space, the bedroom in a lofted area above the kitchen. As Zach said, it wasn't much, crudely furnished with a hodgepodge of artsy and vintage pieces.

"Would you like something to eat? I have—" he pulled open an old refrigerator against one wall "—hot dogs, Pop-Tarts and a frozen pizza."

"That's all right," Kelly said.

He grabbed a Dr Pepper from the fridge and set it in front of her, then got one for himself. Then he retrieved a bag of potato chips from the counter and set them in front of her. She opened the bag and pulled a chip out, then nibbled at it.

"So, what do you think I should do?"

He studied her intently for a long moment. "I'm probably the wrong person to ask."

"Why is that?"

"Because I don't want you to go back to L.A. And anything that might take you back there is bad in my book."

"Even if it means I might be able to have some success in acting?"

He smiled ruefully. "No. That would be pretty selfish of me. I don't think you'd ever ask me to give up my dreams. If you have to go back, I'll understand. And I'll try to let you go. But it's not going to be easy."

"This is silly," Kelly said. "It will all blow over and then I'll be left exactly where I was yesterday. Trying to figure out what I want to do with the rest of my life."

"Maybe we should just decide what to do with the rest of the afternoon."

Going to bed and losing herself in an hour or two of passionate sex had definite appeal. She smiled at him, her chin cupped in her hand.

"We could take a nap," he suggested.

"You don't look tired."

"You could make me tired," he said.

"You know what I'd really like to do? I'd like to get naked and crawl into bed and watch old movies all afternoon."

"You've come to the right place for that," Zach said.

"I figured you wouldn't object to the getting naked part."

"My buddy has shelves and shelves of old classic Hollywood films. All the Bogart films and Hitchcock.

Jimmy Stewart and Katharine Hepburn. What would you like to see?"

"What does he have?"

"Everything," Zach said. "You name it."

Kelly thought about her choice. "Something romantic. *Breakfast at Tiffany's?*"

"Total chick flick," he said. "But one of my favorites."

Kelly threw her arms around his neck and gave him a playful kiss. "After that we'll watch *Casablanca.*"

Zach grabbed her and picked her up, wrapping her legs around his waist. He stumbled toward the bedroom and when he reached the bed, he fell forward. They both bounced on the mattress in a tangle of arms and legs.

"You forgot the potato chips and the soda," Kelly said.

"I'll get them when I grab the movies. I just want to lie here and kiss you for a while, if that's all right by you."

Kelly ran her fingers through his dark hair and smiled. "That's just fine by me." She looked into his eyes. "Sometimes, it feels like we're living in a movie. It doesn't seem real."

"No?" Zach asked. He unbuttoned her blouse and kissed her between her breasts. "Does that feel real?" He pulled aside her bra and playfully licked her nipple. "How about that?"

"I don't know, do it again."

He flipped her over and pulled her skirt up, then gently bit her backside. "How about this?" he murmured.

Zach pulled her lacy panties down over her hip and placed a damp kiss on her skin. This time he focused all his attention on his task and when he turned her back over again, Kelly's pulse had quickened and her breathing was shallow.

"I was mistaken," she admitted. "That feels very real."

"DO WE HAVE TO DO THIS NOW? Can't we go back to bed and do it later?"

Zach adjusted the light diffuser until he found just the perfect balance to illuminate Kelly's face. She sat in a tattered easy chair that he'd pulled into the center of the loft. Sometime in the midst of their movie marathon, after they'd thoroughly seduced each other, she'd slipped into a faded T-shirt and a pair of boxer shorts she'd found in his dresser. They'd laid in his bed, their fingers intertwined, talking about favorite movies and Hollywood stars, films that made them laugh and films that made them cry.

He learned that Kelly was a hopeless romantic, even though she professed to hate sentimental films. They argued about *It's a Wonderful Life* and *Citizen Kane* and *Gone with the Wind*. They debated the acting talents of Gregory Peck and Gary Cooper. By the time they got up to eat the Chinese food they'd ordered, Zach had realized that Kelly knew almost as much about film as he did. Only her knowledge hadn't come from academic study, but from a talent for dissecting an actor's performance.

"Have you ever thought about becoming an acting teacher?"

Kelly wriggled around in the chair until she was comfortable, then placed her hands on her lap. "No," she said.

"Those who can, do. Those who can't, teach. Though I do trade acting lessons for yoga lessons. But I always thought that becoming a teacher would be an admission of failure."

"I don't think so," Zach said. "Listening to you talk, it's amazing how much you know about filmmaking. I'd never even considered some of the things you'd mentioned. You have a very keen insight."

She shrugged. "I just know what I like."

"Do you like me?"

Kelly smiled and sank back into the chair, stretching sinuously, her shirt riding upward, baring her midriff. "Maybe," she teased. "All right, I like you a lot."

He'd always wondered what it might be like to find his creative equal in a woman. None of the women he'd known in his past had had any appreciation for his love of film. But Kelly understood and she was able to talk about it with him, and challenge his ideas, forcing him to look at things in different ways.

Zach had always told himself that he'd need this quality in a woman in order to fall in love with her. Of course, he'd never thought he'd find it. And now that he had, the notion of falling in love with Kelly seemed so simple. Maybe he was already just a little bit in love with her.

Yet, Zach knew she still had a lot of hang-ups about him. He could fall hard only to find out she'd never love him in return. And then, where would that leave him? Loving her would be a huge risk and one he wasn't ready to take. At least, not yet.

While he'd been lying in bed with her wrapped in his

arms, watching *Breakfast at Tiffany's,* he'd come up with a new idea for a film that would use the interviews he'd done with Kelly as a framework for his story about a woman at a crossroads in her life.

Zach had come up with the story a long time ago, but the main character had always been a man, a college professor who had struggled to write the next great novel, and his student, a young woman who had not yet realized the depth of her own talent. But since he'd been interviewing Kelly, the story had taken on a different slant and he'd begun to imagine an alternative version of his script. The main character was now a woman, involved with a younger man.

All the details seemed to fall into place immediately— the scene sequence, the dialogue, the structure. Every conflict suddenly came into sharp focus in his mind, and he was anxious to get started on a rough draft. But he needed to go deeper, to explore the depths of Kelly's dreams and aspirations, her fears and insecurities.

Zach adjusted the camera on the tripod, then looked through the lens. She looked stunning in the soft light, her dark hair and pale complexion almost shimmering for the camera. "Look at me," he murmured.

She turned her gaze toward the camera and smiled sleepily. "All right, what do you want to know this time?"

"Let's talk about celebrity," he said. "Do you remember the first time you thought about being famous?"

"I think it was always there," Kelly said. "I wanted people to notice me. The only time my parents did was when I was on stage. I don't remember when I realized you had to be famous to be noticed. I guess it might have been after I did my second or third play in high school and all the boys started paying attention to me. I played Cherie in *Bus Stop* and it's a very sexy role for a high-school junior and I was very convincing."

"Marilyn Monroe played her in the movie," Zach said.

"And I studied that movie from beginning to end."

"What was that like, the attention from the boys?"

"At first, I was confused by it. They didn't seem to want me, they wanted the girl I played. I was flattered by the attention and so I started to play her offstage, as well as onstage. Or at least my version of her."

"And…?"

"And I realized the kind of power an actress has over her audience, to make them believe in a role so much that they can't separate fantasy from reality. They want the fantasy. And then later, I also came to understand the power that women have over men. Because that's really all about fantasy, as well, isn't it?"

"What do you mean?" Zach asked.

"Men prefer to see women as sexual objects rather than as complete and sometimes flawed human beings. We are the fantasy, the body that was meant to give you pleasure. It's only later, when a man falls in love, that he puts the fantasy behind him and gets to know the real woman. Some men never do get beyond it."

"Do you like sex?" Zach asked.

A pretty blush rose in her cheeks and he was surprised

that she felt embarrassed to talk about it. She was so un-inhibited in bed that he assumed she'd be the same way out of bed. "Sometimes," she said.

"Only sometimes?"

"I haven't always. When it's about two people connecting, communicating without speaking, like it is with you, then I like it a lot. I like the moment when both of us just…surrender. It's like a moment of perfection. But sometimes sex is all about power."

"And what about love?"

She laughed. "What about love?"

"Have you ever been in love?" Zach asked.

She stared at the camera for a long time before answering, a strange mix of emotion flickering in her eyes and over her expression. "I wish I could say yes. I thought I was a few times, but now, I know I wasn't." She sighed softly. "Maybe someday." Kelly paused. "Or maybe not."

"If you could choose—fame or love—which would you take?"

"I don't know. I suppose I can't say until I've had a chance to experience one or the other. I guess the proper answer would be love, but sometimes love is just as difficult to hold on to as fame is. All this fuss about me and my lips, that will all go away on its own, no matter what I do."

"I think your lips are really something."

"Turn the camera off now," she said, putting her hand up to block the shot. "I don't want to talk anymore."

"What do you want to do?"

She stood up and walked toward the bedroom, tugging the T-shirt over her head as she moved. "I was thinking I might want to have sex." Kelly dropped the shirt on the floor, then turned around to look at him.

"With whom?"

She grinned, then shimmied out of the boxers. "Whomever's available. You, if you're up to it."

"You think it's that easy? You just take your clothes off and I'll be there, ready to see to your needs?"

She nodded. "Yes, that's exactly what I think. You have five minutes to decide and after that, I'm going to take a shower." Kelly held up her hand, five fingers outstretched. "I'll be waiting."

Zach stood next to the camera and watched as she disappeared into the bedroom. He imagined her lying down on the bed, naked and ready, her dark hair spread across the pillow. She had such power over him and sometimes it was a bit frightening. Zach had always controlled his relationships, moving forward when he felt good about a woman and retreating once he'd had enough. But with Kelly, he'd become obsessed, determined to possess her at all costs, even if it meant risking his heart.

He'd only made one mistake in his life and that had been Margaret Winters. The woman had been a master at manipulation and he hadn't recognized he was in too deep until it was too late. Had he made the same mistake again?

Zach glanced down at his watch. He'd wait six minutes and then see if she'd be true to her word. Who wanted the other more? Would she wait for him? Or would he give in before the five minutes were over? It was a silly test and one that he'd played often. But it seemed wrong to do it to Kelly.

He turned off the lights and moved them back against the walls, then slid the chair over to its spot near the sofa. When he finished, he walked slowly toward the bedroom. It had only been three or four minutes. He'd surrender this time. But next time, he'd stand firm.

When he got to the bedroom, the bed was empty and the door to the bathroom was slightly ajar. He heard the water running and Zach smiled. So this was how it was going to be. He sat down on the edge of the bed and waited, listening to Kelly as she sang softly. Images of her, her skin wet and warm, slick with soap, danced through his head.

With a frustrated groan, he unbuttoned his jeans and kicked out of them. All right. When it came to Kelly, he'd concede that he didn't possess the power to resist her. In truth, he wasn't sure he even wanted such powers.

He chuckled softly as he stepped into the bathroom. When he peeked inside the glass-block shower, she was standing beneath the falling water, her face turned up, her hair plastered to her back. Without a word, he stepped inside and slipped his hands around her waist.

A satisfied smile curled her lips. "What took you so long?" she asked as he smoothed his hands over her backside.

Zach didn't reply. Instead, he pressed a kiss to the curve of her neck, flicking his tongue against her damp skin. He moved down, licking at her breasts, bringing her nipples to a hard peak, then going lower.

When he reached the juncture of her thighs, he gently turned her around and pressed his mouth to the small of her back. He slid his hands around her legs and gradually moved higher. When his lips reached the nape of her neck, Kelly arched back against him.

He knew her body like he knew his own, every perfect curve, every soft spot. If he pressed his lips below her ear he could feel her pulse, and if he buried his nose in her hair he could smell the familiar scent of her perfume. If he suddenly went blind, Zach could find her among a hundred women, just by touch.

They teased each other with fleeting caresses and warm kisses, touching and testing, every sensation heightened by the warm water. There were times when they were like children, playing with each other, laughing and teasing. And then, their play would turn serious and they'd sigh and moan with pleasure. When she gently sucked on his nipple, Zach leaned back against the wall of the shower and let her take the lead.

With her fingers wrapped around his shaft, Kelly slowly began to stroke him as she continued to explore his body with her lips and tongue. At first, he relaxed into the easy seduction, knowing it would take time for him to reach his climax.

But when she furrowed her fingers through his hair and pulled him into a deep kiss, his desire surged and every stroke of her hand brought him closer. She knew how to touch him, how to keep him close to the edge and aching for release. And it was at times like this that he felt completely vulnerable, as if she held the key to all his desires.

"Oh," he moaned against her mouth. "Don't stop. Just like that."

She took his lower lip between her teeth and bit gently, enough to cause a tiny hint of pain, enough to focus his thoughts on the rush of sensation pulsing through his body.

He tried to hold back, but it was impossible. The warm water, her slick skin and the sweet taste of her mouth were more than he could handle. And in one deep shudder, he let go, bracing his hands against the shower wall as his body surrendered to her touch.

Kelly continued to stroke him until he was too sensitive to continue. Zach grabbed her wrist and stopped her, then groaned softly. He heard her laugh softly and he looked down at her, her hand covered with his essence. "What are you doing to me?" he murmured.

"If you don't know, then we're both in trouble."

She misunderstood, taking his question literally. But, in truth, it was more an expression of his fears. These feelings she evoked were intense and always overwhelming. Yet, he'd come to crave this intimate contact. And like an addict, he wondered what would happen if it were ever snatched away.

Zach had to believe there'd come a time when she would leave. It was the only way he could keep himself from falling in love with her.

THUNDER RUMBLED in the distance and Kelly walked to the front of the store to peer out the windows. The sky had grown dark and ominous clouds slowly moved from west to east. She'd been in Atlanta for almost two weeks and had grown used to the frustrations of the weather. Heat, followed by a thunderstorm, which promised relief but never delivered, and then more heat.

Angie had assured her that though summer was beastly hot, the other three seasons were quite pleasant. With only a week left in August, Kelly wondered whether September would usher in reasonable weather—or whether she'd even be in Atlanta to enjoy the autumn. She'd learned not to think too far into the future. It only made her uneasy. With every thought of the future, came thoughts of Zach.

She'd tried so hard to maintain a pragmatic attitude toward their relationship. At first, she thought it would be simple, just two consenting adults, friends with benefits, and nothing more. But she'd grown to care for him, to count on him. And though they both tried to pretend there was nothing serious between them, Kelly could feel it every time he touched her or looked into her eyes.

This morning, while unpacking inventory, she'd made a list in her head of all the reasons it would never work. Oddly, most of those reasons had come down to the age difference. She'd always hoped that if she found a man to love, he'd want to have children. But Zach wouldn't be ready to start a family for years, and by that time she might be too old.

When she turned forty, he'd still be in his twenties and

probably more gorgeous than he was right now. Every day, she'd be faced with the worry that a younger, prettier woman might come along and steal his heart. She saw how women looked at him on the street and it bothered her.

And she was so settled in her ways, sure of how she wanted to live her life. Zach was still growing up, still learning about the man he'd become. What if he changed as he got older and became someone she couldn't love? Or worse yet, what if he never grew up?

There were other doubts that crept in and out of her head, usually in the moments before she fell asleep in his arms. Was she really ready to let her career go? She couldn't continue to pay rent on an apartment in L.A. while she lived in Atlanta. And sooner or later, Joe would want his condo back and she'd be forced to find a new place to live. One way or the other, she'd have to make a decision soon.

"Hello!" Angie's voice echoed from the back of the store and a moment later, she appeared with two lattes and a bag from a local bakery. They'd agreed to meet and go over the purchase orders for the Christmas merchandise since the store was closed until noon on Sundays.

"Hi," Kelly said, grabbing the coffee from Angie's hand. She took the bag and peeked inside. "Blueberry bran muffins?"

"Yum." Angie flopped down in one of the leather chairs and stretched her legs out in front of her, sipping at her coffee. "Looks like we're going to get a big storm," she said. "Joe is home with Caroline. Whenever she hears thunder, she freaks. She slept with us last night and the night before, thus these lovely bags under my eyes."

"You look fine," Kelly said.

She shook her head. "I can't believe I'm going to do this all over again." Kelly frowned and Angie looked up at her and smiled weakly. "I'm pregnant."

"What?" Kelly gasped.

"I missed my last two periods and I thought it was stress, with all the stuff that's been going on with the new store. And then I thought it was the heat. I even convinced myself I was going through the change. But I peed on a stick this morning and I'm going to have a baby."

Kelly sat down next to Angie and took her hand. "This is good news, right?"

Angie nodded, tears swimming in her eyes. "It took me two years of trying to get pregnant with Caroline. And we've been hoping to have another child. I'd pretty much given up and then surprise, surprise!"

"What does Joe say?"

"I haven't told him yet. He's going to be thrilled but he's also going to have some concerns—mostly about the new store."

"But that will be done before you have the baby, won't it?"

"That's what I need to talk to you about," Angie said. She drew a deep breath. "I need to know if you're going to stay in Atlanta. If you aren't, then I have to start looking for someone to manage the stores while I'm having a baby. I know you're not ready to make a decision, but if I have to train someone, I need to start soon. I was in bed the last four months of my pregnancy with Caroline and I'd assume that will happen again."

"When do you need to know?" Kelly asked.

"Soon," she replied.

Kelly drew a ragged breath. "Maybe you should find someone else. It's not that I don't love working here, because I do. But I don't know what I'm going to be doing or where I'll be living in a few months." She groaned and lay back in the chair, staring up at the ceiling. "Sometimes, I think I should just go back to L.A. until I'm ready to decide."

"What's in L.A.?"

"Nothing," Kelly said.

"Exactly. Here you have a job and a place to live and a boyfriend. And what about all that interest stirred up at the football game?"

"I'm not going to be the woman who has a career based on her lips! That's just too…shallow. If they want me for my acting talent, then fine. But not my lips."

"Maybe this isn't about the job or your lips or finding a new place to live. Maybe this is about Zach."

"How could it be about Zach? I've known him for two weeks. How could it possibly be about him?"

"Because, you're falling in love with him and it scares you," Angie said.

Kelly sat up and shook her head. "I'm not. I'm doing everything in my power *not* to fall in love with him." She cursed softly. "It's just getting really hard to do."

"We don't choose who we fall in love with," Angie said. "If we're very lucky, love chooses us."

Kelly glanced over at her friend and fought back a surge of tears. "I said that to you. The night you told me you were going to leave L.A. and move to Atlanta to be with Joe."

"It was the best thing you could have said to me. It made me realize how lucky I was to even find him in this crazy world. If you're meant to be with Zach, then nothing is going to keep you apart, especially not eleven measly years."

Kelly smiled. "You know, I figured for five months out of the year, we'll only be ten years apart. That's not quite as bad, is it?"

"No," Angie said, her voice filled with optimism, her expression bright. "That's much better!"

Kelly couldn't help but laugh at Angie's reaction, and before long, they were both in stitches, the tears running down their faces, their breath coming in gasps. "You really are a good friend but you're a horrible actress. If you're going to lie, you need to learn to do it more convincingly," Kelly said.

"I know," Angie replied. "But I just didn't have time to get in to character. Besides, I never was a very good actress anyway."

"Neither was I," Kelly said.

They both burst out in another round of laughter and Kelly realized how much she'd miss this if she went back to L.A. This was one thing she could put in the Pro column. Atlanta had Angie, a wonderful friend and her only confidante. But was that enough to tip the scales?

"Can I have a few more days to think about it?" Kelly asked, brushing a tear from her eye.

Angie nodded. "As long as you're considering it, then Joe should be satisfied. He just gets all worried if he thinks I'm doing too much. And the last time I was pregnant, he was a bag of nerves. He drove me crazy."

"It must be nice," Kelly said. "To have someone watching out for you."

Angie got to her feet and held out her hand to Kelly. "Come on, let's get out of here. I don't want to do inventory today and I certainly don't want to eat those blueberry bran muffins. There's a Waffle House out on the interstate. Now that I'm pregnant, I can eat whatever I want and I want pancakes and sausage, drenched in syrup, and I want scrambled eggs and ham and hash-browned potatoes and a big glass of orange juice."

"All right," Kelly said. "Let's go."

They dodged raindrops as they ran out to the car. By the time they got on the interstate, they rain was coming down in sheets. Kelly opened the car window and stuck her face out, letting the rain whip at her cheeks and hair. "Do you remember that old car we used to have? Mabel."

"It was a 1985 Buick LaSabre," Angie said. "I bought it with that money I made doing that episode of Buffy. Three thousand dollars. What ever happened to that car?"

"I sold it to a guy for four hundred bucks," Kelly said. She held her hand out the window, letting the rain hit her palm. "If I decide to stay, I'm going to have to go back and pack up my stuff. I can fit most of it in my car, but I'll probably have to rent a U-Haul if I want to bring any furniture."

Angie glanced over at her and smiled. "I'm sure that Sweet Nothings would help pay for your moving expenses."

"I'm still not decided yet," Kelly said, "but I'm seriously considering it."

"Well, wait until you've eaten at the Waffle House," Angie said. "You'll just have to move to Atlanta then. Joe brought me on my first trip to Atlanta and I was convinced that any place that had fifty different kinds of waffles was a place I needed to live."

"I thought it was that big old diamond ring he gave you that sold you on the idea of marrying him."

"No," Angie said, "it was definitely the buttermilk waffles at the Waffle House."

Kelly gave her a playful shove. "See, the acting chops come right back once you start using them."

"I'd like to thank the Academy and my agent and manager. And all the fans that've meant so much to me over the years. Oh, and my best friend, Kelly Castelle, who always believed in me."

Kelly smiled to herself as she stared out the window. Maybe Atlanta could be home after all. Once she brought her things out from L.A. and set up housekeeping, maybe she'd feel more settled. She wouldn't know until she tried.

7

THE DREAM WOKE HER UP from a dead sleep. Kelly rubbed at her eyes and tried to remember what it was about. She'd been on a beach and someone had been chasing her. It had been dark and the sand kept slowing her down. She knew there had been more to it, but all she was left with was a faint feeling of terror.

She reached over to touch Zach, but his side of the bed was cold and empty. Kelly pushed up on her elbow and turned on the light, then rubbed her eyes again as she glanced around the room. They'd come to his apartment after having dinner together and as soon as they'd closed the door behind them, they'd torn off their clothes and tumbled into bed.

She smiled to herself. When it came to sex, Zach seemed to have an insatiable appetite—and the uncanny ability to tempt her with just a boyish smile or a silly comment. There would probably come a time when their sex life became routine, but Kelly couldn't imagine it happening anytime soon. She still found him irresistibly sexy and devastatingly handsome. And to her delight, he seemed to think she was the most beautiful woman he'd ever known.

She smiled and snuggled beneath the bedcovers. It had been two days since Angie had asked her for a decision and Kelly was almost ready to give her one. They'd discussed salary and Kelly had looked at a few apartments in midtown. As predicted, the furor over her JumboTron appearance had died down. Her fifteen minutes of fame had lasted approximately five days. No one had been able to find her and she'd managed to move around Atlanta, disguised only in Angie's huge Gucci sunglasses.

Lonely for company, Kelly grabbed a T-shirt from the end of the bed and tugged it over her head. She found Zach at the dining table, his laptop screensaver illuminating the room in the dark. His head rested on his arms and he was sound asleep, papers scattered all round him.

Kelly grabbed a stack and quietly straightened them, then looked at them more closely. Recognizing the format of a script, she found herself curious as to what Zach was working on. She gathered the rest of the papers and walked over to the easy chair, switching on a nearby lamp.

By the time she'd put them all in order, the first light of dawn was brightening the windows of the loft. She settled back and began to read. The first four pages were a treatment, a short synopsis of the story meant to hit the main themes and outline the beginning, middle and end.

As she read, an uneasy feeling grew in her stomach. His script was about an older woman...a college professor who'd never realized success as a writer. She'd become involved with a younger man, a writer who'd shown promise with his first manuscript. From there, the story veered sharply from her own as the professor began to manipulate the young man in a bizarre quest for the fame that had eluded her.

It was emotional and intense and wonderfully written, a story of sexual obsession and professional envy. As Kelly read through each page, she realized how talented Zach really was. He could have a wonderful career ahead of him in films. And given the proper representation, this film could go from an independent project to a feature film with bankable stars.

But her admiration for his talent didn't mitigate the feelings of betrayal she felt. He'd used her. She'd been…research. There were bits of dialogue scattered throughout the script, things she'd said to Zach in conversation and on tape, fears and insecurities. Private thoughts he was planning to share with the world.

She let the script fall to the floor, the pages floating in every direction. He had no idea what he'd done, no clue as to how this made her feel. She'd become a modern-day Norma Desmond, that pathetic creature in *Sunset Boulevard,* madly in love with a younger man who'd promised to make her a star again. Sure the setting was different, a small college town instead of Hollywood, but the story was exactly the same. Zach must have seen the parallels and known how it would make her look.

And then the heroine goes mad. Was that what he expected from her? Did he believe that one day, she'd suddenly crack and see him as her enemy instead of her lover?

Kelly brushed a tear from her cheek, then got up and

walked back to the bedroom. She couldn't stay here, couldn't face him in the morning. It had been easy to forget the difference in their ages, especially when it seemed as though it didn't matter to him. But after reading the script, Kelly knew that he was acutely aware of the years separating them. It was one of the central themes of his film. And for his hero and heroine, there was no happy ending.

She slowly got dressed, gathering her clothes from the floor and numbly pulling them on. She slipped into her shoes and turned for the door, only to find Zach standing in front of it, his arms braced on either side of the doorjamb.

"Where are you going?" he murmured in a sleepy voice.

"Home."

Frowning, he ran his fingers through his mussed hair. "To the condo?"

"Yes." She swallowed hard. "And then, back to L.A."

Zach took a step forward, suddenly wide-awake. "What are you talking about?"

"I read your script," she said. "It's very good."

"Thank you," he replied, a suspicious look fixed on his face. "Is that why you're upset?"

"What do you think?" Kelly asked, her voice laced with sarcasm. "You took my life and turned it into a movie. You took conversations that we had and turned them into dialogue. How am I supposed to feel?"

"All writers base their work on real life," Zach said.

"Besides, this is just the rough draft. By the time it's finished, you won't recognize anything."

"Is that supposed to make me feel better?"

He crossed the room and tried to grab her hand, but she stepped around him and began to make the bed. "Damn it, Kelly, what's the big deal?"

"You used me for research. The woman you've been sleeping with. Was that all part of the plan, to make me feel comfortable with you so that you could get more out of me?"

"Don't be ridiculous."

"And the thing that really bites is that you didn't even bother to tell me you were writing a script about me."

"It's not about you," he said. "It's just…it's about what you're feeling, what you're going through. You know, coming to a crossroads in your life and not knowing which way to turn. Lots of people go through the same thing, Kelly. It's universal, that's why it makes such a good story."

She hitched her hands on her waist, refusing to look at him. "I want to go home. I want you to take me back to the condo."

"No," Zach said. "We're going to talk about his until we get it straightened out. Until you understand."

"I don't want to talk about it." She stalked out of the bedroom and he followed hard on her heels. When she got to the kitchen counter, she grabbed his keys. "If you won't drive me, then I'll take your truck."

Zach tried to snatch the keys from her hand. He caught her wrist and held it, prying them from her fingers. "I'll take you home after we've sat down and talked this out."

"I have nothing to say to you."

"Well, I have something to say to you," Zach countered. He pointed to the easy chair. "Sit."

Kelly was tempted to defy him, but if she didn't do as he asked, he'd never take her home.

"I didn't go into this thinking I'd write a script about you," Zach said. "It was only after the last conversation we taped that I came up with the idea. The things you said about being a celebrity and what it meant touched something in me. So I started writing and I wrote this all in the past two days."

"I don't believe you," Kelly said.

"It's true. I've been writing after you fall asleep and I've been writing while you were at work. It all just came out and I couldn't seem to stop it. It had to be written. I was just the typist here, Kelly. You were the inspiration, the muse."

"It's *Sunset Boulevard*," Kelly said.

Zach scoffed. "No, it's not. It's about a crazy, obsessive woman who couldn't let go of her dreams, who'd do anything to make them happen. That's not you. You've left L.A. behind. You knew when to let go. This character can't let go."

"And you think I can? Angie offered me a job managing one of her stores and I couldn't give her an answer. Deep in my heart, I still think there might be a chance to do what I've dreamed about doing."

Zach shook his head. "I thought you'd already decided to stay," he murmured.

"No," Kelly said. "In fact, I've pretty much decided to

go back." She knew the words would hurt him and she saw it in his eyes—the shock, the pain. A flood of guilt surged up inside of her and she wanted to take it back, but her anger had overwhelmed her consideration.

"Because of this?" Zach held up his hands. "Don't try to sell me that story, because I won't believe it. Be honest, for once. This is just an excuse. Hell, you've been waiting for an excuse to end this since it started."

"That's odd coming from you, a man who keeps all kinds of little secrets. You want me to be honest? Why don't you try doing the same?"

"All right, let's be honest. The story isn't entirely about you. It's about a woman named Margaret Winters. I had a very brief affair with her last fall. She was a dean at the university I was attending, but I didn't know that when we got involved. She was twenty years older than me and I was flattered that she found me fascinating. And I stupidly started seeing her. When things fell apart, she found a way to cancel my grad-school grant and I was out. Two years of work toward a degree down the tubes, all because I refused to keep servicing her."

"So, I'm not your first older woman?"

"No," he said in an emotionless tone. "The character is based on her, but you gave her a voice, you made her sympathetic. You're not her in body, Kelly. Just in soul. And I deliberately wrote her that way so that you could play her."

Kelly stared at him for a long moment. "You wrote the part for me?"

"Yes. As I wrote it, I pictured you in the role. I'm planning to produce and direct it, so I can choose who I want to play that role. And I want you."

"Is that what you plan to use all your millions for?"

This brought him up short. He shook his head. "You know about the lottery?"

Kelly nodded. "That's another thing you didn't tell me."

"I didn't think it was important," he said with a shrug. "Besides, I don't have the money yet. And it looks like it might be a while before I get it."

"You didn't trust me," she said.

"Maybe I didn't trust myself," Zach said. "Believe me, the moment you started talking about going back to Cali, I was going to bring it up. I figured it was my ace in the hole. How could you possibly walk out on a guy with millions?"

"Is there anything else you've neglected to tell me?"

"Yeah," Zach said. "There is one more thing."

"I can't wait."

He reached out and grabbed her hand, lacing his fingers through hers. Then he tipped her chin up until she met his gaze. "I love you."

"No," Kelly said, clapping her hands over her ears, "don't say that."

"It's true. From the moment I first saw you, I was in love."

She stared at him for a long moment, then shook her head. "I have to go. If you won't take me, then I'll call a cab."

"Don't do this," Zach warned. "Don't be so quick to throw this away."

Kelly took the keys from his hand and walked to the door. "I'll wait for you in the truck."

When she reached the safety of the hallway, she leaned back against the door and drew a deep breath. Isn't this what she'd expected to happen all along? If it was, then why did it feel like she'd just torn her heart in two? This was for the best. It never would have lasted anyway.

"It's for the best," she murmured as she walked down the hall. It would just take a little time for her to convince herself of that fact.

ZACH SAT BEHIND the wheel of the truck, parked in front of Kelly's condo. After a long, silent ride home, she'd hopped out and run inside, without even looking back.

He stared out the windshield, unable to understand how things could have gone so bad so fast. He'd never meant to hide anything from her, nor had he thought his script would cause her any distress at all. But then, he really didn't know Kelly Castelle that well, did he?

It hadn't been a week since he'd realized she was still in Atlanta and since then, they'd spent nearly every free moment together. At first, it had been all about the sex, and Zach hadn't considered that a problem. But lately, they'd been getting to know each other in a much more intimate, emotional way.

Hell, he should have known it would end badly. Every relationship he'd ever been in ended badly. Still, considering what had happened with Margaret Winters, this didn't rank right up there with the worst.

He suspected she wasn't really angry about the script. She knew Hollywood as well as he did, if not better. And as an actress, she used her life experiences all the time in preparing for a role. He used his in writing a script. And everything that had passed between them had been shared, hadn't it? Zach cursed softly. All right, maybe it was a little selfish for him to assume she'd be all right with it. He'd just been so caught up in creating the story that he'd never thought any further than getting it down on paper.

Cursing softly, Zach turned off the truck. This wasn't over until they both decided it was over. And as far as he was concerned, he wasn't ready to give up. He hopped out and ran to the door, then punched the security buzzer.

"Go away," she said.

"Come on, Kelly. We're both adults. We can discuss this without all this dramatic bullshit. Let me in. At least give me a chance to apologize."

There was a long silence and Zach leaned up against the door, holding on to the handle. Then, after nearly a minute, the door clicked open. He strode inside and up the stairs to her place. The door was open a crack and he pushed it inward.

She stood in the middle of the foyer, watching him warily. She looked so sad that Zach wondered if he had the words to make her feel better, to make her smile. He crossed over to her in a few long strides and captured her face between his palms, kissing her gently.

"I'm sorry," he murmured, pressing his forehead against hers. "I'm stupid. I'm an idiot. I should have asked you before I wrote word one. God, Kelly, I'd never deliberately hurt you, you have to know that."

She stared up at him and smiled tremulously. "I'm sorry for being such a bitch."

"You aren't. You had every right."

"It's a good story," she said. "And it doesn't matter how you came up with it."

"You really think it's good?"

She nodded. "I do. And it would be a wonderful part, for a woman…my age."

"You know that I don't think about that, not when you and I are together. It doesn't make a difference to me."

"Not now. But someday it will."

Zach closed the door behind him, then took her hand and led her to the sofa. He pulled her down to sit on his lap and then kissed her again, wrapping her in his embrace. "Are you really going to leave?"

"Yes," she muttered. Then she drew a ragged breath. "I don't know. Maybe. I feel like my life has gone right off the rails and I can't seem to get it back on."

"What's wrong with it?" Zach asked. "You're living in a great city, you've had a wonderful job offer, you're dating a real prince. And he's got pretty good prospects. And he's madly in love with you."

"Zach, you can't be in love with me. You've only known me for a couple weeks. You're in love with the sex, not with me."

"I know how I feel," he said. "Just because I'm younger doesn't mean—"

She put her finger on his lips to silence his words, then leaned forward and kissed him. "All right," she murmured. "I do believe you."

"So where do we go from here?" Zach asked.

"I don't know. I guess, until I decide where I'm going, we won't know where we're going."

Zach smoothed his hands through her hair, pushing it away from her face so he could look into her eyes. "I want you to be happy," he said. "If it's with me, then that would be great. But if you have to go back to L.A. to be happy, then I'd understand. But until you figure things out, I still want us to be together. If we only have a week or even a few days, I want to spend them with you." He dropped a kiss on her lips. "Is that all right?"

She nodded, then threw her arms around his neck and kissed him. Zach molded her mouth to his, enjoying the sweet taste of her, the scent that he'd come to know so well.

"I have to get to work, but I'll call you later and we'll go out and get some dinner."

"I'll be at the store. Call me there," she said.

Zach kissed her on the forehead, then stood. He wanted to grab her and carry her off to the bedroom, stripping off her clothes along the way. He needed proof that things were still right between them, that she still wanted him as much as he wanted her. And he needed to lose himself in her body, to feel that deep connection that came when he made love to her. But for the first time since they'd been together, he resisted the impulse.

It took all his willpower to walk to the door, to admit

that making love to her wasn't going to fix their problems. He glanced back over his shoulder and she gave him a wave before he stepped outside. As Zach strode back to his truck, he bit back the frustration.

It was all a lie. He wouldn't be happy if she went back to L.A. The only thing that would make him happy was if Kelly stayed in Atlanta, with him, for as long as he was here. Damn it, he had a right to be selfish, didn't he? They were so good together and she just refused to see it. And maybe it was an immature attitude, but he didn't want to give her up.

When he got back inside the truck, he closed his eyes and tried to make some sense of what was happening. None of his experiences with women had prepared him for this. He'd always thought when he finally fell in love, he'd know what the hell he was doing. But he was at a complete loss as to how he could make things work between them.

Maybe he ought to encourage her to go back to L.A. After all, he didn't plan to stay in Atlanta for that much longer. Once he'd collected his lottery winnings, he could head out to the west coast and join her. And maybe, by then, she'd have realized that she couldn't live without him.

Zach smiled. Somehow, he wasn't so confident that that would be the case. Kelly had been with other men before and had managed to leave them behind and move on with her life. What made him think that he'd be any different? If anything, she'd be more anxious to put him in her past, considering her hang-ups about his age.

He started the truck and headed toward the studio. Jeff had decided to take a few days vacation and Zach was covering the editing duties while he was gone. He had one show to edit in the morning and another to tape in the afternoon, but then he'd be free to see Kelly.

By the time he rolled into the parking lot it was nearly eight. He grabbed a pop from the fridge and wandered back into the editing suite. Cole was already waiting, watching raw footage as he sipped a cup of coffee.

"You're early," he commented.

"Sorry. I've had some things going on. But I'm turning over a new leaf."

Cole gave him a strange look. "Let me guess. Woman problems?"

"Are there any other kind of problems?"

"Sure. But then, you don't have kids, so you don't have to worry about those problems yet. Just wait, that will come later."

"How much trouble can two seven-year-old girls possibly be?" Zach asked. "They don't date yet, do they?"

"No!" Cole replied. "And if I have anything to say about it, they won't until they're twenty-one and trained in the martial arts."

Zach chuckled. "Oh, you're exactly the kind of father that all young men hate."

"Good. They should fear me." He leaned back in his chair. "I knew it was going to be hard, raising them on my own. But I never expected to get tripped up by such silly things. We had a big argument the other day about makeup.

Schuyler said that all her friends wear makeup to school. I gave her the old 'if your friends jumped off a bridge' speech. Then, she asked when she could wear makeup and I didn't have an answer."

"Don't look at me," Zach said. "All I know is that the girls I've dated are always messing with their makeup."

"They ought to publish an owner's manual for fathers with daughters. They're much more difficult than sons."

"Hey, they ought to publish one for grown women, too. I'd buy that book in a heartbeat."

"So, what's the problem?" Cole asked.

"You really wanna hear about it?"

He nodded. "Sure. Maybe I can offer some advice based on my limited experience."

"I've been seeing Kelly Castelle. You know, the—"

"The girl with the lips," Cole teased.

"Yeah. Believe me, she's a whole lot more than just lips."

"I gotta tell you, I'm impressed with your game," Cole said. "I wouldn't have had the nerve to make a move on her. A woman like that is way out of my league."

"I'm starting to think she's outta mine, as well," Zach said.

"Maybe you should keep your options open," Cole suggested. "You're coming into a lot of money for a young guy and you never know what the future holds."

Zach shrugged. "Maybe you're right." He took a slow breath and shook his head. "I'm trying hard to figure this out. It shouldn't be this difficult."

He reached out and hit Play on the console, ready to get to work. Maybe he'd just have to resign himself to the fact that he couldn't control the future. Whatever happened would happen and he'd have to accept it for what it was. Hell, Cole had been married and his relationship had failed. If things were going to go bad with Kelly, it would be better that it happened before they'd put more time into it.

It sounded good, Zach mused, but he still couldn't get behind the notion that they wouldn't end up together. If she left, he'd probably find a way to get over her. But it would take a long time before he forgot her.

"CAN I INTEREST EITHER of you in dessert?"

Zach didn't bother to look at the waiter. Instead, he stared at Kelly, sitting across the table from him, dressed in a sexy black slip dress that clung to her body like a second skin. From the moment he'd picked her up at her condo, he'd been fantasizing about what she had on under the dress. He'd also wondered why, after a two-day separation and a pact to put a bit more distance between them, she'd chosen a dress that would make him want to crawl all over her.

Mixed signals, he mused. From any other woman, he might get irritated. But from Kelly, it just made the evening more interesting. Would they go their separate ways after dinner or would they end up where they always had, in bed, making love?

Kelly glanced up at the waiter and smiled. "I'll have dessert. And a cup of coffee," she said.

"I'll bring the dessert tray," the waiter offered.

She turned back to Zach, folding her linen napkin and setting it on the table. "Dinner was wonderful."

He'd picked the most elegant restaurant in all of Atlanta and then begged Eve to put in a call and get them a reservation. He'd even gone out and dropped over a thousand on a suit, shirt, tie and shoes, in an attempt to impress her. He wanted Kelly to see him as something more than just a struggling filmmaker. In a few months, he'd be a millionaire.

"I've missed you," he murmured.

She shook her head. "It's only been two days."

"Have I told you how beautiful you look tonight?" he asked.

"At least five or six times," Kelly replied. "You're pretty handsome yourself. I like the suit. It makes you look…older."

"That's kinda what I was going for," he said. "I even combed my hair. See, I can roll with the big boys. I'm cool, I got my sexy on." Kelly giggled, and he reached across the table and grabbed her hand, lacing his fingers through hers. "This is nice. I'm glad we're still okay."

"We are," Kelly said.

"Yeah, we are." He smiled. "I have to tell you, things were getting pretty intense there for a while. But, I think it's good that we took a step back."

"I know," Kelly said. "Everything has moved so fast since I got to Atlanta. And it was really difficult to get a handle on it all when we were so…infatuated. I suppose it's that way at the beginning of every relationship."

"But now, things are good, right?"

The waiter returned with the dessert tray and explained the selections. Zach waited for Kelly to choose. "I'll have the crème brûlée," she said. "No, wait, maybe I should have the tiramisu. I love tiramisu."

"I have no idea what either one of those are," Zach said. "But why don't you bring the lady both of them?"

"No!" Kelly cried.

"Yes. I'll just share your dessert."

"All right." She looked at the waiter. "Bring them both." Zach grinned as she glanced back at him, a playful wince on her face. "That carrot cake looked really good, too."

"Should I call the waiter back?" Zach asked.

She shook her head. "So, how is the script coming along?"

"Good," he replied. "I'd like you to read it again. I'd like your opinion."

"I'd like to read it."

"And I'm serious about you playing the lead. I mean, if you want to. It'll probably be a long time before I even get it into production, but I'm writing it for you, so you should play it."

In truth, it was a way to keep them connected, a way to assure him that even if she did leave town, they'd see each other again. Over the past couple days, Zach had tried to convince himself that he could live without Kelly. And he'd almost accomplished that, until he'd seen her again.

The attraction was still so intense, the need so overwhelming. And though she tried to play it cool, he knew she was feeling the same thing. The passion between them hadn't disappeared. It was like a bubbling pot, its cover rattling and its contents ready to boil over at any minute.

But did he want to turn up the heat? Was he willing to force the issue and make her see how much she wanted him? Or would it be better to just switch off the heat and let it go?

"I think your story has a lot of potential," Kelly said. "And maybe you'll want a bigger name for the lead. If a major studio picks it up, they'll probably have someone in mind. And that's all right. I'd completely understand." She paused. "You're going to have to make some compromises."

"I know." He studied her face, taking in each perfect detail. Her image had been burned indelibly into his brain and Zach knew he could never completely forget her. Two years from now, five years, even, she'd be there, fluttering through his dreams.

"And sometimes it's going to be really difficult. But it's all part of the game out there."

The waiter arrived with the desserts and Zach had him place them both in front of Kelly.

"Do you want to try?" she asked. Kelly dipped her finger into the dish and scooped out a bit of the dessert, then held it out to Zach, tempting him. She could have used a spoon and he wondered what made her use her finger. "Try it."

He stared at her finger. "What is it?"

"Crème brûlée. The smoothest, richest custard you'll ever taste. With burnt sugar on top."

"Custard?"

"Come on, try it. You have to expand your horizons."

He shook his head warily. "I don't know. I'm a Pop-Tarts kind of guy. Ice cream. Pie. The occasional donut." He leaned forward and reluctantly took her finger into his mouth. He smiled as he pulled back, his gaze fixing on hers. "That's really good." He licked the end of her finger.

Kelly pulled her hand away and Zach saw her tremble slightly. "See, I told you."

"I'll eat that one," he said. She wasn't quite as cool as he thought she was.

"No, you have to try the other one." She scooped out a bit of the tiramisu. "This has ladyfingers and mascarpone and espresso and—"

"I don't know what any of that stuff is," Zach said. "Well, I know espresso. But ladyfingers? What the hell is that?"

"Little cakes that are shaped like fingers," Kelly explained. "Come on, try it."

This time, when he took her finger into his mouth, he gently sucked on it, leaving no doubt how he felt about her little taste test. "All right. I get it. That was really good." He reached out and scooped a bit onto his finger and held it out for her. "I can see that you're going to need to teach me to be more adventurous with my eating."

"I guess it's a good trade-off," she said.

"For what?"

"For you teaching me how to be more adventurous in bed," Kelly murmured, her cheeks growing pink with a pretty blush. She licked the dessert off the end of his finger, then handed him a spoon and the tiramisu. "Did I tell you about Angie? She's going to have a baby."

"Really," Zach said. "That's nice."

"Yes," she murmured, nodding. "It is. I'm happy for her. She's wanted to give Caroline a brother or sister for a long time. I'm glad it worked out for her."

"Do you ever think about having kids?" he asked.

"Sometimes. I haven't put any serious thought into it. I think I'd want to have a man in my life, probably be married. A lot of women in Hollywood have babies on their own, but they have the money to be able to hire nannies and pay for doctor bills and baby clothes and private schools and big houses with nice yards. Those of us with limited finances don't have as many choices." She took another bite of the dessert. "That's what I hate about Hollywood. It's not about the acting. It's about the money. Sometimes I think I should go back to New York and try my luck there."

"New York is great. I could live in New York. I did live in New York. But I didn't have money then."

"After you get your millions, you can live anywhere," Kelly said.

"I could. I could live in Paris or Rome or Hong Kong. I could live where you live," Zach said.

She sent him an enigmatic smile. "You could," she answered.

He reached out and grabbed her hand. "Why don't we get out of here?" Zach helped her to her feet, then tossed some cash on top of the check. They walked out into the warm night and strolled hand in hand to Zach's truck. It was a perfect August night in Atlanta, not too hot with a slight breeze in the air.

Zach rolled the windows down and they drove back to midtown listening to the Braves game on the radio. When they reached Kelly's condo, Zach pulled up at the curb and turned off the ignition. "Maybe we should go out for a drink or something," he suggested.

"I've got a bottle of wine inside," Kelly offered.

It was an invitation, and not just for a drink. He could see it in her eyes. Zach nodded, then hopped out of the truck and circled around the front. He grabbed Kelly by the waist and lifted her down, then walked with her to the front door.

When they got to her condo door, Zach grabbed her wrist and gently pushed her back against the door, the key jangling in her hand. He bent close and brushed a tender kiss across her lips. When he drew back, she was watching him with wide eyes.

"I've been wanting to do that all night," he murmured.

"I've wanted you to do that all night," she countered.

"Yeah?"

Kelly nodded, then reached back and unlocked the front door. Zach held on to her waist as they walked inside. The moment the door clicked closed, he spun her around in his arms and kissed her again. His fingers furrowed through her hair as he moved her mouth against his. She tasted sweet, like the dessert they'd shared.

Any attempts they might have made to try to put distance between them had now failed miserably. There was no fighting the attraction. Kelly grabbed the lapels of his jacket and pulled them over his shoulders, then began to work at his tie. Zach allowed her to undress him as he continued to kiss her. When she'd stripped off his shirt and removed his belt, she pulled him along to the bedroom. But Zach stopped her halfway down the hall, pinning her against the wall and drawing her leg up along his hip.

The silky fabric of her dress wasn't much of barrier to his touch. He could feel every soft curve of her body. Zach pulled the skirt up along her legs, bunching the fabric in his fists. Then he slid his hands around her backside and picked her up, wrapping her legs around his waist.

He was hard and hot, his erection pushing against the fabric of his trousers. Every time she moved, he felt his desire build. His hands skimmed over her body, frantic to touch her. Zach's fingers tangled in the tiny straps of her dress and he pulled them down and trailed kisses along her shoulder.

Kelly arched back, sighing softly as he gently sucked on a spot near her collarbone. When he grabbed her legs again, she wrapped her arms around his neck. Then he carried her into the bedroom and lowered her to the bed. Leaning over her, he ran his palm from her chest to the sweet spot between her legs, the silk slipping past his fingers.

Zach wanted to go slow, but he couldn't seem to stop himself, and Kelly wasn't helping. She reached for his trousers and undid them, sliding the zipper down and then skimming them over his hips. He'd worn boxers and she did away with those, as well.

She seemed determined to seduce him and Zach had no intention of stopping her. There wasn't an hour in the day that he didn't want her, that he didn't fantasize about the next time they'd be together, naked, lost in each other's arms. And he wanted to believe that she felt the same overwhelming desire for him, that there were times when she couldn't control her need. It was the only thing that held them together but it was powerful and it was real.

When she'd finished with his clothes, she pulled the dress up over her head and tossed it aside. As Zach had suspected, she was wearing nothing underneath except a sexy black thong. Just the sight of her pushed him closer to the edge and when she reached out to touch him, he stepped back. "Don't," he murmured. "Let me touch you."

Kelly lay back on the bed and Zach kicked off his shoes and socks, then stepped out of the rest of his clothes. He sank down on the bed beside her and then slipped his hand around her waist. Slowly, he began to kiss her…her neck, her shoulder, the soft tops of her breasts. He teased at her nipple with his tongue before drawing it into his mouth and gently sucking. She moved in his arms, stretching sinuously as he worked his way lower, to her belly and then her hips.

When he found the spot between her legs, he flicked at the damp slit of her sex with his tongue. She cried out, her fingers clutching the bedcovers. He slowly seduced her with his mouth, taking his cues from her soft moans and her quickened breathing. Before long, she was wild with need, begging him for release, but Zach was patient. He didn't know how much longer they'd have together, and from now on, he was going to make it wonderful between them, an experience she couldn't easily forget.

He teased her for a long time and then he grabbed his trousers and pulled a condom from his wallet. He'd been hard from the start and when she sheathed him, he held his breath, ignoring the waves of sensation that raced through him at her touch.

She pulled him down on top of her, settling him between her legs, then twisted beneath him. The tip of his shaft probed at her damp entrance and he slipped inside of her, then pulled out. "Please," she murmured. "I need you so much."

"God, I need you, too," Zach said. His jaw tensed as he entered her again, slowly burying himself deep inside her. For a long time, he didn't move, enjoying the warmth surrounding him. But the temptation was just too great and when she arched beneath him, he moaned and pushed deeper.

Their rhythm was slow at first and Zach focused on the scent of her hair, the feel of her skin beneath his fingers. Sex had always been fun and playful between them. But this was different. There was an edge of desperation to their coupling. He couldn't seem to get close enough, deep enough. With every stroke, Kelly arched against him, moaning softly.

He kissed her again, hungry for the taste of her, running his hands through her hair. There was nothing about her that didn't make him crazy with desire. Zach pushed up, bracing his weight on his arms, then gently pulled her toward the edge of the bed.

He stood up and wrapped her legs around his hips. She lay on the bed, naked to his view and as he continued to plunge into her, he watched her. Pleasure suffused her expression and she looked at him through passion-glazed eyes, her lips swollen from his kisses.

She was beautiful, everything he'd ever wanted or needed in a woman. And when he was with her, he felt complete, as if all the pieces of his life had come together in a single, exquisite place. Zach reached down and touched her again and Kelly's eyes closed as she focused on his caress.

A soft moan slipped from her throat and he felt the first of her spasms. It didn't take much to put him over the edge, and when her body shuddered and her orgasm consumed her, Zach let go. The feel of her tensing around him was more than he could take, and he collapsed onto the bed, driving into her one last time. He gasped for breath, his body shaking as his orgasm peaked and then subsided.

"There," she murmured, gently running her fingers through his hair. "That's better."

How would he ever do without this? If she left him, then he'd spend the rest of his life searching for this feeling again, this overwhelming sense of completion. It didn't matter what the future held for him. He just had to be sure Kelly was a part of it.

Zach had to believe there was a chance for them. He realized it was the only thing that he'd ever truly wanted in his life and he had to find a way to make it happen.

8

KELLY GLANCED AT her watch and then picked her cell phone out of her purse. It was nearly 10:00 a.m. west coast time and she knew Louise didn't get into the office before nine. She'd been thinking about calling all morning, trying to decide what she'd say and how she'd say it.

Louise had always been a cheerleader of sorts, keeping Kelly's spirits up when jobs were few and far between. And she'd always been a believer in Kelly's talent as an actress. But now it was time to have a heart-to-heart, and Kelly hoped that Louise would be honest with her. She'd ask her point-blank if it was worth returning to L.A. for her career. And if Louise said no, then it would finally be over.

She drew a steadying breath, her heart racing, as she dialed the number on her cell phone. But to Kelly's dismay, the call went through to voice mail. She left a message, asking her agent to call her back as soon as possible.

Kelly put the phone back inside her purse but the minute she pulled the zipper shut, it rang. She glanced at the caller ID and recognized the L.A. area code. "Hello?"

"We must be on the same wavelength," Louise said. "I was just going to call you."

"You were?"

"To say that you should have called me!" Louise scolded. "Why didn't you tell me about your little appearance during that football game on ESPN?"

"I—I didn't think it was important."

"Well, all the buzz has gotten back to L.A. and casting agents have been talking. One of them matched your headshot with the footage on ESPN and called me to set up a meeting. I have to tell you, I didn't know what he was talking about, the girl with the lips."

"It was silly. I'm not going to build a career around my lips."

"Well, you won't have to. Your lips just managed to get you in the door, but your talent is going to have to keep you there. You've just been offered a job on a new series on Fox."

"An audition?"

"No, they want you. You'd be a regular. No audition."

Kelly gasped. "What's the part?"

"Well…now, don't take this the wrong way but…"

"Don't tell me they need a hooker," Kelly muttered.

"A mother," Louise said. "You'd play the mother of sixteen-year-old twin boys. It's one of those teen series and they have some hot young actors attached and from what I can see, it's going to be a big hit. Three, maybe four seasons at the least and you'd appear in nearly every episode in the first two seasons."

"Oh, my God," Kelly said. "A series?"

"They'd like to meet with you next week, introduce you

to the twins. They're not teens, by the way, so don't worry about working with kids. They're twenty-three. But they look young."

"Twenty-three," Kelly murmured. That was just a year younger than the man she'd been sleeping with! Suddenly, all her doubts came crashing back in. Though she wasn't old enough to be Zach's mother, she was old enough to play her on TV!

"How old am I?" Kelly asked.

"Actually, you had them when you were eighteen. It's a whole high-school romance, pregnancy thing. Thirty-four. Now, I have to talk to you about salary," Louise said. "They're offering twelve thousand."

"For the whole season?"

"Per episode," she replied.

"Oh, my God. That's…what?"

"A quarter million. But I'm thinking if we let this ESPN thing play out a little longer, I might get them to raise their offer to fifteen thousand an episode. Once I start making some calls there might be other offers. Bigger things."

"No," Kelly said. She drew a calming breath. "No, let's just wait. I need to think about this."

"You need to come back to L.A.," Louise insisted. "The show will start as a midseason replacement and then have a full season in the fall. They film in Vancouver, but we'll work out an agreement to get you back and forth to L.A. when needed."

"Wow. This is all so unexpected."

"They want you here by Monday for meetings and then they start production in late October."

"All right," Kelly said. "Listen, I'll call you back this afternoon. And yes, you can go out there and market me as the girl with the lips. But I'm only taking decent parts, nothing trashy, all right?"

"I knew if we were just patient, things would turn around for you," Louise said. "It's your time. We have to take advantage of it."

"Yes," Kelly said. "I'll call you later." She closed the phone and set it on the counter, then took a deep breath and screamed as loud as she could. Jumping out from behind the counter, she did a happy dance in the center of the store.

Angie appeared from the storeroom, a concerned look on her face. "What is it? Are you all right?"

"No," Kelly said. "I'm just…stunned. I just talked to my agent. I've been offered a television series."

Angie's expression fell. "Really? A series?"

"Not just a guest spot, a regular role. I guess all the buzz about me here has reached Hollywood. My agent has been getting calls all morning. They want to meet with me. I don't have to audition. They want me!"

"What are you going to do?"

"I'm going to take it," Kelly said. She frowned. "I mean, I think I'm going to take it. Why wouldn't I? It's a great opportunity. And the money is fantastic."

"It is a great opportunity," Angie said. "And you have to take it."

Kelly stared at her friend for a long moment. "I'm sorry."

"Don't you dare be sorry." She circled the counter and gave Kelly a fierce hug. "I will always be here and so will the store. And if you ever want to come back, there will be a job waiting for you."

"I will come back," Kelly said. "To visit."

"What about Zach?" Angie asked.

Kelly drew a deep breath and sighed deeply. "I don't know. We'll just have to see on that one. He'll be here in Atlanta for a while yet, but after that, we might find ourselves in the same city."

"You act like it will be so simple to leave."

"It should be," Kelly said. But she knew it wouldn't be. These last few days with him had been strange. Since their night at the restaurant, their relationship had changed. There was a bittersweet edge to it now, as if they'd both accepted the fact that there might be an end coming soon. The attraction was still so powerful, and the sex, fierce and frantic. But the world they'd created for themselves, the fantasy that had been impervious to the outside world, was now vulnerable.

"But it won't be," Angie countered.

Kelly shook her head. "No, it won't." She groaned. "I tried so hard to resist him. I thought I could do this, just have a casual affair and then walk away. I never expected to feel this way."

"Then do something about it," Angie said.

"No." Kelly stepped out from behind the counter and

shook her head. "I need to go back and give this a shot. On my own. Until I'm on my own again, I'm not going to know how I really feel about him. We're still so obsessed with each other that I've convinced myself I can't live without him—or without the sex." Kelly smoothed her skirt. "I'm supposed to meet him for dinner tonight and I know that it's going to turn into a huge scene. I'd just rather tell him and get it over with and then we can get on with our lives."

"Do you really think it will be that easy? He's in love."

"He thinks he's in love," Kelly corrected. "What does he know about love?"

"What do *you* know about love?" Angie asked. "Not much more than he does." She grabbed Kelly's purse from beneath the counter and handed it to her. "Tell him now. If he really loves you, then he'll be happy for you and you'll find a way to be together." Angie handed her the car keys. "You can take my car."

Kelly stared at the keys. Why was she so anxious to talk to Zach? Was it because she wanted things to be over between them? Or was it because she wanted reassurance that, no matter how far apart they were, there'd still be a chance. Zach wasn't going to live in Atlanta forever. And maybe they could make things work with a long-distance relationship.

If he were in love with her, truly in love, then he'd have to support her decision to take the job. "All right," Kelly said. She glanced at her watch. "They're taping a show this afternoon, but maybe we can go out for a quick lunch…or brunch."

"Go," Angie insisted.

Kelly hurried out the back of the store and found Angie's car parked in its usual spot. As she got inside and started the ignition, a nagging sense of indecision came over her. Yes, Zach would have to support her decision— because she wasn't giving him any option.

Though Kelly hadn't been back to the station since her second day in Atlanta, she knew where to find it. She parked in a visitor's spot in the lot, then hurried to the front door. As she walked through the lobby, the receptionist looked up and smiled. "Miss Castelle!"

"Hello," Kelly said.

"You're early. But that's all right. I'm sure Nicole will want to talk to you before the show."

"Nicole?"

"I'll just buzz her and she'll be right out."

Kelly frowned. "But I'm not here to see—"

"Just have a seat," Mindy said, as the phone trilled again.

Kelly waited patiently to correct her, but the phone kept ringing. This would be embarrassing, Kelly mused. But when Nicole appeared at the security door, there was nothing to be done but explain her presence.

"Kelly! Gosh, I wasn't expecting you. I spoke to Zach a few days ago and he said you wouldn't be interested. But I guess he convinced you."

"Interested in what?" Kelly asked.

"In appearing on the show. We're taping 'In Praise Of Younger Men' this afternoon." She paused. "That's not why you're here?"

"No," Kelly said, "I came to see Zach. I—I need to talk to him. I thought I was done taping the skit."

"After I found out you and Zach were seeing each other, I mentioned to him that I'd like you to appear on the show, as a guest. I thought it would be a wonderful hook and with all the publicity surrounding your appearance at the Falcons game, Atlanta will be interested."

"You know about that?"

"Of course. One of the guys from the studio recognized you."

"No, I meant about me and Zach."

Nicole shook her head. "Well, not directly. He said you were dating. And considering his late arrivals at work, I just put the two together. Even if it were just casual dating, we'd love to have you on our panel. Please say you will."

"I really just came here to talk to Zach," Kelly said.

"You don't even have to sit on stage," Nicole offered. "We'll put you in the audience. You can stand up and offer your experiences that way."

"I'm not sure Zach would want his personal life discussed on television."

"Then we won't even mention the fact that you two are involved."

Kelly winced. "I'm just not comfortable with that. Sorry."

"Then would you agree to talk to me, one-on-one? I think your input would help us frame our topics more effectively."

Kelly thought about her request. Nicole could have fired her after her outburst that first day, could have sent her packing back to L.A. with her reputation in tatters. But she'd given Kelly a second chance and because of it, Kelly had met Zach. She owed Nicole at least this much. "All right."

"Come on. Eve is in hair and makeup. I want you to talk to her, too."

Kelly followed Nicole back into the production offices and when they got to the hair-and-makeup room, they found the host of *Just Between Us* in the midst of getting her hair blown dry. Eve glanced up from the note card she was reading. "Hello! How are you?"

"Fine," Kelly said.

"I have to tell you, I think your work with Zach on those segments was just wonderful. Anyone watching would have to think that you two have a real thing for each other."

"Actually, they do," Nicole said. "Kelly has been dating our Zach for the past couple weeks."

"Really," Eve said, with a mixture of disbelief and interest. "And I suppose Nicole has brought you here so you can tell me all about it. We are going to put her on the show, aren't we?"

Nicole shook her head. "She doesn't want to appear on camera. But she's willing to give us an interview. I thought another viewpoint might be interesting, especially since we know the younger man in question."

Eve pointed to the chair next to hers. "Sit. Let's talk. Tell me about your relationship."

Kelly drew a deep breath. "Well, I guess I should start by saying that all the preconceived ideas you may have about older women and younger men might be true for some couples. But for other couples, they aren't. At the beginning, I thought age would make all the difference. And now, I realize that it doesn't make any difference at all. We were just two people trying to find something in each other that we hadn't found in anyone else."

"Were?" Eve asked. "As in past tense?"

Kelly shrugged. "I don't know. Maybe. I have to go back to L.A. this weekend. That's why I stopped by, to tell Zach."

"Tell me," Eve said. "If you and Zach would have been the same age, would you have stayed? Would you have asked him to come with you?"

"No. Because we wouldn't have been together in the first place. I think the reason we were together was because I needed someone who saw things differently than I did. Who saw me differently than I saw myself."

"He made you feel young?"

Kelly shook her head. "No. He made me feel… ageless." She chuckled. "Which is better than feeling young."

"I really wish you'd agree to be on camera," Eve said.

Kelly shook her head. "No."

"What about if you call in?" Nicole suggested. "We'll put you in the control booth and if you have something you like to add you can just pick up the phone. Eve wears an earpiece and we'll let her know that you want to comment. It would be strictly anonymous."

"Why is it so important that I do this?"

"Because, you, more than anyone, know about the obsession with youth and beauty," Eve said. "You can juxtapose that with your interest in a younger man."

Kelly drew a deep breath, then sighed. "All right. As long as it's anonymous. I suppose that wouldn't be a problem."

"We start taping in a half hour," Eve said. "Nicole, why don't you get her set up in the control room?"

Kelly glanced around and forced a smile. How did she get caught up in this? She'd come to the station to see Zach, and now she was preparing to reveal intimate details about their relationship. She bit her bottom lip. Well, she wouldn't do it. They couldn't force her to speak, could they?

"HERE YOU ARE!"

Zach glanced up from the editing console to see Nicole standing in the doorway, clutching her clipboard. "What can I do for you?" he asked.

"You know how I wanted you to invite Kelly to be on the show today?"

Zach groaned inwardly. "Yeah."

"You didn't ask her, did you?"

"No. I knew she wouldn't do it."

"Well, you were wrong," Nicole said. "She's going to do a call-in. And I think you should do a call-in, as well. Just so you can give the male point of view."

Zach slowly spun around in his chair to face her, his brow furrowed into a frown. "She's really going to be on the show?"

Nicole nodded. "I just set it up. So, what do you say?"

"I say, I want to talk to her before I agree to anything."

"Nope," Nicole said. "I don't think so. Either you're in or not. You can talk to her live during the show."

"This is bullshit," Zach said, jumping to his feet.

"This is talk television," Nicole countered with a grin, "and I have a show to produce. Yes or no?"

Zach frowned. Was Kelly really ready to discuss their relationship on the air? And if she were, what would have prompted such a decision? Something had happened and he needed to talk to her right away. If Nicole wouldn't tell him where she was, then he'd just have to find her.

The phone rang in the editing suite and he picked it up. "Zach Haas."

"You've got a visitor waiting out front," Mindy said.

Zach smiled. "Kelly Castelle?"

There was a long silence on the other end of the line. "No. Some guy in a suit. He wouldn't give me his name."

"I don't know any suits," Zach said.

"Well, you must because he asked for you specifically. He claims it's a personal matter." She lowered her voice. "I don't think he's a cop."

"I'll be out in a second." He pointed to Nicole. "You wait here. We're going to talk." Zach strode out the door and made his way through the maze of hallways to the reception area. He pushed the door open and stepped out, crossing the lobby to the only guy wearing a suit.

"I'm Zach Haas," he said.

"Yes, Mr. Haas. I'm Elliot Dunlop. We spoke on the phone."

"The lawyer from New York?"

He nodded, then reached into his breast pocket and withdrew a card. "My firm is representing three male students from City University in New York. They've all brought a lawsuit against Dean Margaret Winters."

"I really don't have time for this," Zach said. "I'm in the middle of something and to be honest, I'm not interested."

"Mr. Haas, we've tracked down a number of alumni who had had some problems with Dean Winters, as well, and they've agreed to be party to the lawsuit. But we need solid proof. With your case, we have it. Dean Winters wrote a letter to your dean, asking that your grant be revoked. And if you tell the jury about your affair, then they can't ignore the obvious."

Zach raked his hand through his hair. "Why should I do this?"

"Why not? You were harmed. You weren't able to finish your degree. Your investment in your education was lost. You deserve to be compensated."

"You sound like a commercial."

"Think about it. Take my card. I'll be here in Atlanta until tomorrow morning. My cell-phone number is on the card. Call me and we can discuss this when you have more time."

"All right," Zach muttered. "Maybe." He glanced at his watch. He was due in the studio in ten minutes. The audience would be seated in five and the preshow warm-up would start right after that. He reached into his pocket, grabbed his cell phone and dialed Kelly's number. But after three rings he got her voice mail.

"You will call?" Dunlop said.

"Yeah," Zach said. "I have to go."

He waited as Mindy buzzed him back into the production offices, then dialed the number of Sweet Nothings. Angie picked up the phone. "Hi, Angie. It's Zach. Is Kelly there?"

"Hey, Zach. No, she's not. She took my car and was going to see you at the studio. She left a half hour ago. Maybe she had to make a stop along the way."

"Thanks. If she calls you, can you have her call me right away on my cell?"

"No problem," Angie said.

He snapped the phone shut, then returned to the editing suite. Nicole was waiting for him. "So you'll do it?"

"Yeah. If she's doing it, I'll do it."

"Good. I'll have Larry cover camera three. You can watch the feed from the show in here. Call the control room from the phone and we'll patch you through. And please, be interesting. I want this show to be fantastic."

Zach sat back down at the editing console and picked up the phone. Cole answered and Zach explained what Nicole had planned. "All right, Zach," Cole said. Zach listened to the hum of voices over the telephone as Cole got the show rolling. "Let's make it a great show, people. Eve Best to the studio, please."

The next fifteen minutes were filled by a warm-up, which consisted of Eve fielding questions and comments from the audience. Usually a comedian or one of the producers did the warm-up, but this was what Eve did best and every now and then, a lucky audience got to enjoy it. As Zach listened distractedly, he waited for Kelly to call. He even double-checked his cell phone to make sure it had a signal and battery life.

The show seemed to move grindingly slow, probably because Zach was used to watching from behind camera number three. He paid special attention to the segments that he and Kelly taped, pleased with the way they turned out. They were already thirty-five minutes into the taping when he heard Nicole's voice over the phone. "All right, we're going to do the phone interviews in forty seconds."

He watched the clock as the seconds ticked down and then focused on Eve's voice.

"And we're going to go to the phones," she said. "We have Sylvia on the line right now. Sylvia is a thirty-five-year-old actress who is involved with a twenty-four-year-old man. And, no, we're not talking to Demi or Cameron today. Sylvia, welcome to *Just Between Us.*"

"Thank you." It took only two words for Zach to recognize Kelly's voice. "It's nice to be here."

"Let's talk about your younger man. What makes him different from the older guys you've dated?"

"To be honest, it isn't his age that makes him different," Kelly began. "I think I was just lucky to find a man who understood me. He just happened to be twenty-four."

"And when you first met him, did you think his younger age was a positive or a negative?"

"Both," Kelly said. "I mean, obviously every woman would like to think she's attractive to younger men. But then again, I wondered what I could have in common with him."

"Let's talk to Sam now," Eve said. "Sam, how did you feel when you met Sylvia?"

"Sam?" Kelly said.

"Hello, Sylvia," Zach replied. "I'll tell you Eve, I was smitten."

Eve laughed. "Smitten?"

"Yes. Completely. Sylvia was beautiful and any guy, young or old, would have been attracted to her. Besides, I didn't think she was that old."

"How old did you think I was?" Kelly asked.

"Thirty," Zach replied. "How old did you think I was, Sylvia?"

"Twenty-seven," Kelly said. "At least that's how old I hoped you were."

Eve cut in. "For two people who aren't hung up on age, you seem to be worried about it now."

"Hey, I've never been hung up on her age. She's the one with the hang-ups."

"I don't have hang-ups," Kelly said. "I'm simply old enough to recognize the practicalities of a relationship with a younger man."

"And what are those practicalities?" Eve asked.

"Well, it's usually all about him," Kelly said, her voice edged with sarcasm. "This is a problem. He wants me to stay in Atlanta because this is where *he* is, where *his* job is. He's never once offered to live where I want to live."

"Until this minute, I thought you did want to live in Atlanta," Zach said. "When did that change?"

"So I sense a conflict here," Eve said, stating the obvious. "Do you two argue often?"

"No!" they both said at the same time.

"I'd just like to know why she thinks I wouldn't live

where she wanted to live," Zach said. "She's never asked me to move."

"Let's move on to your sex life," Eve suggested.

"Let's not," Zach said. "I want to talk about this. Tell me, Sylvia, do you have plans to leave Atlanta?"

"Yes," Kelly said. "And if I asked you to come with me, would you come?"

"Where are you going?" Zach asked.

"I don't know. Maybe Los Angeles. Maybe the moon. What difference does it make?"

"I'd consider it," Zach said.

There was a long silence on the other end of the line. "Well, Sylvia, what do you say to that?" Eve asked. "Audience, we'll hear Sylvia's answer when we come back."

Zach exhaled forcefully. Even waiting a few seconds to hear what Kelly had to say was torture.

"And we're back," Eve said, a moment later. The space for commercials would be added in the edit. "Well, Sylvia, you've had a few minutes to think about this. Are you going to ask Sam to go with you?"

"I think we'll have to discuss it a bit more," Kelly said.

"So there is hope for this December-May romance," Eve said. "And now I'd like to introduce our final guest, Dr. Sara Miller, who has written a book called *The Myth of the Younger Man*."

Eve's voice disappeared from the phone line and Cole came on. "Thanks, you two. Nice work."

"Where are you?" Zach asked.

"In the control room," Kelly replied.

"Meet me in the lobby." Zach hung up the phone and headed to the front door of the studio. He met up with Kelly in the lobby, then grabbed her hand and walked out the front door. When they reached his truck, he unlocked the door and helped her inside. Then, he hopped behind the wheel and started the ignition.

"Where are we going?"

"I don't know. It's too hot to sit in the truck while it's idling. And I need to get out of here."

For a long time, they didn't speak. Zach headed toward Piedmont Park and when they arrived there, he parked the truck beneath the shade of a maple tree. "I can't believe Nicole talked you in to that."

"I figured I owed her for my screwup that first day. And I didn't expect it would turn into an argument. I just thought I'd say a few nice things about you and that would be it." She glanced over at him. "I'm sorry."

Zach studied her, his gaze searching her features for some sign of how she really felt about him. He knew she cared, it was written all over her face. "Have you really decided to leave Atlanta?"

Kelly nodded. "I talked to my agent this morning and I've been offered a role in a new television series."

The news hit him like a punch to the gut. She was leaving. "Wow," Zach murmured. "That's fantastic."

"I know. And the strange thing is, the offer came off all that buzz from the football game. Can you believe it? They're even talking about that out in L.A. Louise thinks there will be other offers. I guess I have you to thank for it all."

"I think that's great," Zach said. And he did, deep inside. He wanted Kelly to be happy and if going back to L.A. and continuing with her career would do that, then he'd be happy for her. But that didn't mean he couldn't be frustrated for himself. "And who knows? Once I get the money from the lottery, we might be on the same coast again."

"Maybe," Kelly said. "Except the series shoots in Vancouver."

"I hear Vancouver is great," he said. "Not a bad place to live, either."

"It's good that it worked out this way," Kelly said softly, staring down at her fingers.

"Yes," Zach murmured. "I mean, it was silly to try to make plans for the future when neither one of us knew where we'd be in a six months."

She nodded. "You could be anywhere in the world with all your millions."

"I could be back in grad school in New York," Zach said.

"You're considering that?"

"Maybe," he said. "It seems silly not to finish. I've only got a semester left. And I just found out that some lawyer is bringing a lawsuit against the dean who cancelled my grant. So, if I want to go back, they'll have to let me in."

"I think you should do it," Kelly said.

"And you're sure you're going to take the job?"

"It's a lot of money. More money than I've ever made. And it could lead to other work and who knows? Maybe another series or a movie."

"Of course. You're good," Zach said. "People will recognize that."

"It's funny," Kelly said, laughing softly. "I spent the last ten years worrying about getting too old. And now, all of a sudden, I'm old enough. I'm going to be playing someone's mother."

"You're going to leave soon?" Zach asked, knowing the answer already.

Kelly nodded. "Tomorrow, if I can get a ticket. My agent wants me back in L.A. by Monday."

"You'll let me take you to the airport?"

A tiny smile touched her lips. "Sure. That would be nice."

"And maybe we could have dinner tonight?"

She hesitated before answering, and Zach chided himself for even asking. He should have simply showed up at her door that evening and she wouldn't have been able to refuse.

"It was difficult enough to make this decision, Zach. I think dinner might not be a very good idea. Besides, I need to clean up the condo and check to make sure I can get a flight out. And I want to see Angie again. We'll see each other in the morning."

"We're being so civilized about this," Zach muttered. "It's hard to believe we ever cared about each other."

"We did," she whispered, reaching for his hand and lacing her fingers through his. "We still do. Enough to know when it's time to live our own lives, apart from each other."

"Will we see each other again?" Zach asked.

"Maybe," Kelly said. "Who knows?"

Zach slipped his arm around her shoulders and pulled her close, pressing a kiss to her forehead. To do any more would be tempting fate. He wanted to kiss her, deeply and completely, to try to prove to her that he really did love her. He could even say the words, but Zach knew she wouldn't believe them. And he wanted to hear those words from her in response.

The men in Kelly's past had obviously taught her to be wary of love, to take her time before declaring what was in her heart. She wasn't the kind of woman to believe in love at first sight and if he said the words, it would only make him seem naive and…desperate.

He'd have to accept her leaving for what it was. An end. They'd been moving toward this moment from the very instant they'd met. It wasn't supposed to work and strangely it had—for a little while. But now, it was time to put this one-night stand in the past and to live their lives in the real world, instead of in the fantasy they'd created for each other.

"I should get back to the studio," Zach said.

"And I've got Angie's car. She's going to wonder where I am."

And that was all there was to it, Zach mused as he drove back the route that he'd come. He couldn't feel sad. In truth, he was pretty much numb to any emotion at all. He'd probably begin to realize what he'd lost in a few days or a few weeks. But for now, he'd focus on what he'd had, the woman he'd loved, for two beautiful, steamy weeks in August in Atlanta.

KELLY HAD LEARNED to deal with goodbyes very early in her life. Her father was always off on one medical convention or another. And her mother, after a particularly loud fight, would desert the family for a week or more while she rested her nerves at an expensive spa.

Family had come and gone and so had friends. Men had mostly gone, and now, she was preparing to say goodbye to someone she'd never expected to miss. Zach stood next to her at the airline counter as the clerk made the changes to her ticket and collected the penalties for the flight change.

Up until this moment, she'd thought about changing her mind, about refusing the offer of the series to stay in Atlanta and begin a new life. But she'd maintained her resolve and once she'd changed her plane ticket, there was no going back.

"I'm checked in," Kelly said. "I guess we could go get something to eat. That is, if you'd like to wait." She shook her head. "I'm sorry, I shouldn't have assumed you would."

"I'll wait," Zach said with a shrug.

Kelly took her ticket from the agent, then picked up her overnight bag from the floor. Zach grabbed it from her hand and they walked toward the atrium. Kelly found a place to sit while Zach got them both a cup of coffee at a nearby restaurant.

When she'd left Zach at the studio the previous afternoon, Kelly had thought that she wouldn't see him again before he picked her up at the airport. But around eleven last night, the front door buzzer had rung at the condo and she'd let Zach in. He hadn't said a word to her, just took her hand and led her into the bedroom, then crawled into bed with her, fully clothed.

She'd lain awake for a long time, knowing he wasn't sleeping, either, aching to reach out and undress him, to make love one last time. But there was nothing more to be said between them, no reason to talk. And losing themselves in sex wasn't going to make their goodbyes any easier. So they'd just enjoyed their last hours together, wrapped in the warmth and closeness that had grown between them.

When the sun came up, they'd crawled out of bed and gathered Kelly's things, then walked down to the truck. She'd looked out the window as they drove away from the condo, wondering if she'd ever see Atlanta again. And if she'd ever see Zach again.

Kelly watched as he approached with the coffee, fighting back a surge of emotion. It was strange to think they'd part and then simply go on with their lives, never thinking of each other, not knowing what the other person was doing. Someday he'd meet another woman and he'd fall in love and marry her and have beautiful children. If there was a woman out there for Zach, then there had to be a man out there for her.

She'd be happy, too. Maybe her career would take off and maybe she'd find contentment there. Until now, she'd always had to fight for every job, competing with actresses who always had more training or more experience, prettier hair or bigger boobs. And though she'd always believed she was perfect for every part, the rejections got to be hard on her ego. But this was proof. They wanted her and nobody else.

Zach handed her the coffee, then sat down beside her. "I guess you'll be happy to get back home, to sleep in your own bed."

She glanced over at Zach. "If you think I'm happy leaving you, you're wrong. I've grown very fond of you. I've become…attached."

"Just say the word," Zach murmured, staring into her eyes.

"Word?"

"Tell me you want me to come with you. I'll go buy a ticket and get on that plane for L.A. with you. That's all it would take, Kelly. Just ask me and I'll go."

She stared down at the paper cup she held in her hand, her thumb circling the lid. "I'd like to," she said.

"What's stopping you?"

"I don't know. It just doesn't feel right. I think I'd be asking you for the wrong reasons."

"And what would those reasons be?"

"Security. Knowing that you'd be there if I fail. Knowing that I can fall back on our relationship if I can't make this new job work. That wouldn't be fair to you. I have to do this by myself. If I know you're going to be there, then maybe I won't try as hard."

"And if you fall and I'm not there to catch you?" Zach asked.

"Then, I'll pick myself up and get on with my life."

Zach reached out and slipped his fingers through the hair at her nape, gently pulling her closer. He pressed his lips to her temple. "You're not going to fall. You're going to be great and this job will open up all kinds of new doors for you."

Kelly touched his face, smoothing her hand over his cheek. "Thank you."

They sat next to each other in silence, holding hands and sipping their coffees. Kelly didn't want to say more, afraid Zach might make some grand gesture and insist on coming with her even if she refused. It was safer this way, to just quietly walk away.

Kelly glanced at her watch. If she expected to make her flight, she'd have to leave now. She slowly stood. "It's time for me to go."

"I know." Zach pushed to his feet and slipped his hands around her waist. "I guess this is it."

She nodded, forcing a smile. "It is."

"If I tell you that I love you, it won't make a difference. If I ask you to marry me, you'd refuse. And if I went over to the counter and bought a ticket, you'd tell me not to come. So, I'm just going to say goodbye and wish you luck and then walk on out of here." He paused. "But I do want you to know you can call me, anytime, day or night, and I'll be there for you."

He cupped her face in his hands and kissed her, gently

and sweetly, until Kelly felt the tears begin to flood her eyes. She'd never known anyone as wonderful as Zach, as kind and as caring. And chances were, she'd never forget him.

When he finally pulled back, Kelly drew a ragged breath, then reached down and picked up her overnight bag. "Goodbye, Zach." It took all her willpower to walk away. When she got to the security checkpoint, Kelly glanced back over her shoulder, expecting to see him there. And when he wasn't, her heart ached.

He'd be all right. And so would she. This was exactly what she'd intended that first night that they'd spent together. It was possible to have a physical relationship and then just let it go. What she hadn't expected was the emotional attachment she developed for Zach. It was sad to walk away and it was sad to think that she'd never see him again.

But then, he'd said he'd always be there. He was just a phone call away. Kelly set her purse and her bag on the conveyer belt, then emptied her pockets into the small basket. She passed through the metal detector, then stood and numbly answered the questions of the security guard.

When he finally waved her through, she continued on down the concourse. With every step she took, Kelly felt as if she were walking away from something she'd never have again. But then she focused on what was waiting for her in L.A. A job, maybe a career. She'd concentrate on work and she'd do what she'd always wanted to do—act.

And in a few months, she'd come to the realization that she'd made the right choice.

"It'll just take a little time," she said to herself, pasting an optimistic, albeit painful, smile on her face.

9

KELLY SAT ON the balcony of her apartment, her feet tucked beneath her, a script for *Twin Oaks Road* spread out on her lap. She'd been back in L.A. for six weeks now and had been caught up in a whirlwind of work. Besides the new series, she'd read for two commercials, a voiceover for a new animated feature and had been contacted by a modeling agency. From where she sat, her career had suddenly shifted into high gear.

Unfortunately, her personal life hadn't left the garage. Though Kelly had plenty of acquaintances in L.A., there was no one like Angie. They had talked two or three times a week since Kelly had returned, discussing Angie's pregnancy and Kelly's work. Joe and Zach. It was a friendship that Kelly hadn't missed until she discovered it again. And now, she didn't want to let it go.

Though she'd tried to put thoughts of Zach out of her head, Kelly had come to the conclusion it was probably better to just allow herself to think about him and talk about him. Thanks to the tapes Angie sent, she'd even taken to watching *Just Between Us,* scanning the audience for the cameramen at the beginning of the show and at the commercial breaks.

She glanced at her watch. Grabbing her mug and the script, she walked back inside. Oreo cookies and coffee were the order of the day when she was watching. She sat down on the end of the sofa and flipped the television on with the remote.

Munching on a cookie, she pressed Play and waited for the familiar theme music. The titles dissolved to a shot of the studio audience. Kelly sat up, peering at the screen. He wasn't in his regular spot. Kelly frowned. Was he sick? Maybe he was just on vacation. Or maybe he'd left the show.

"Hello, everyone," Eve Best said as she walked through the audience. "You're going to love our topic for today. 'In Praise of Younger Men.' We're going to find out whether younger men are really all that as boyfriends and lovers and husbands."

Kelly groaned, then switched off the video player. She didn't need to see this episode again. She'd lived it. Scrambling off the sofa, she searched for her cell phone. Angie answered at the store.

"Hey, it's me."

"Hey," Angie said. "I'm getting slammed here at the store. Gosh, I wish you were still working. I'm tired and I'm starting to get morning sickness and I need my best friend to tell me I don't look like a big marshmallow."

"You look lovely," Kelly said. "I can tell by your voice."

"Hey, I saw you on *Just Between Us* this morning. They ran your episode again. You and Zach were so cute to listen to."

"I was just watching the tape you sent," Kelly said. "But I had to turn it off. I couldn't bear to see it again."

"Aw, sweetie," Angie said. "Do you miss him that much?"

"No," Kelly said. "Well, maybe a little. Lately, I've been so tempted to call him and tell him everything that's going on. But then I think it's best to leave things the way they are."

"I ran into him yesterday. He was picking up lunch from a sandwich place just down the street. He asked about you and I said you were great. Very busy, though."

"How did he look?" Kelly asked.

Angie hesitated, a short silence on the other end of the line. "To tell you the truth, he looked…young. I mean, whenever I saw him with you, you guys looked like a couple. But now that I see him alone, I just can't believe how young he looks. His hair is longer and he hadn't shaved in a few days. And he was wearing those cute cargo shorts that hug his butt and—"

"All right," Kelly said. "That's enough."

"I could call him and tell him you say 'hi' and then maybe he'll call you and you can say 'hi' to each other—without me."

"We're not in junior high," Kelly said with a laugh. "I'm a grown woman. If I wanted to talk to him, then I'd call him myself."

Kelly's call waiting beeped. "I've got another call, Angie. Hang on." She clicked in. "Hi, this is Kelly."

"Kelly, Louise DiMarco. I have wonderful news."

"New wonderful news? Or additional wonderful news?"

"Exciting news. You're up for a part in a film. An independent film, but a film. They want to see you later this week."

"What kind of film? Are they sending a script?"

"It's not finished yet," Louise said. "But they're not going to want you to read. The producers and the director want you to meet with them so they can discuss the role."

"Will it fit into my schedule with the series?" Kelly asked.

"They'll make it fit. Now, they're sending a plane ticket and I'll have it sent over to your place when I get it."

"A plane ticket? The meeting isn't in L.A.?"

"No," Louise said. "Of all places, it's back in Atlanta."

"Who makes movies in Atlanta?"

"Well, the music business is hot there. My guess is that someone from the recording industry is probably financing this. So, what would you like me to tell them?"

Was she really ready to go back to Atlanta? And if she went, would she be tempted to call Zach? And if she called Zach, what would happen? Oh, God, this was a mess already and she hadn't even left L.A. "Louise, can I call you right back? I'm going to need some time to think about this."

"I need to get back to them today," Louise warned.

"Call you back." Kelly clicked back into Angie. "Guess what?"

"That was Zach," Angie said.

"No. Better. I've just had a call to meet with some film-makers in Atlanta. They want to fly me out there next week."

"You're coming back to town?" Angie screamed in the phone. "We're going to have lunch. And we'll shop and go to dinner. And I'm redecorating the nursery and you can help me pick out new wallpaper and paint. You have to let me know exactly when you'll be coming so I don't schedule myself to work at the shop."

"So you think I should take the meeting?"

"Of course. Why not? At the least, it's a free plane ticket to see your best friend."

"And what should I do about Zach? If I'm in town, I really should make an effort to see him."

"Yes, you should."

"But I'm not sure that I want to. I'm afraid if I do see him, things will get out of hand and we'll just end up in bed together, like we did the first time."

"Well, now," Angie said, "that would be horrible. Can you imagine? The two of you, tearing off each other's clothes and rolling around on the bed, naked and sweating and all worked up. Oh, my God. Just the thought of it makes me cringe."

Kelly laughed as Angie's tone grew more and more sarcastic. "Don't make fun of me. I'm serious."

"So am I. Maybe you two should get together. At least I wouldn't have to listen to you moan about how you can't stop thinking about him and how you wish that he'd call and how none of the men in L.A. are as sweet as he is."

"Am I that bad?" Kelly asked.

"No. But I can tell how much you miss him. And after six weeks, if it hasn't gone away, at least a little bit, then

I'm not sure it will. So maybe you need to do something about it."

"Maybe I will," Kelly said. "But if you see him again, don't tell him I'm coming."

"All right. I have a customer, so I have to go. Promise you'll call me back when you get your itinerary."

"Promise," Kelly said. "I'll talk to you later, Angie." She hung up the phone, then closed her eyes and flopped back onto the sofa, kicking her feet up on the back.

This was a strange turn of events, she mused. Almost like fate stepping in and leading her back to Zach. She'd never been a strong believer in fate. People made their own destiny and occasionally luck played a role. But perhaps this was all meant to be.

If she did return to Atlanta, then she'd have to know exactly how she planned to proceed before she landed at the airport. There were decisions to be made. Was she willing to indulge in another one-night stand? Or would they simply have a nice lunch together and say goodbye again? There were so many ways it could go, depending on Zach's reaction to her visit.

He hadn't even attempted to call her in the weeks they'd been apart. Maybe he'd moved on and found another girl, someone living in Atlanta, someone young and pretty. Kelly drew a deep breath. If that's what had happened, then she could deal with it. Or, she could go to Atlanta and not see him at all, thus eliminating the chance that she'd even know for sure.

She had a week to prepare, a week to make a plan. And

a week that would be spent thinking about nothing but Zach Haas—about his sexy smile and his gorgeous eyes and his incredible body. About how he'd made her feel, how he'd touched her and seduced her.

In a week, a lot of things could change—including her feelings for the man she'd tried so hard not to miss.

THE PRODUCTION OFFICES of ATL Video were located in an industrial park outside Atlanta. Zach had worked as a free-lance cameraman for the outfit on a number of hip-hop-video shoots and when he'd asked to use their conference room for an afternoon meeting, they were more than happy to agree.

It had been weeks since he'd last seen Kelly and in that time, he'd finished his script and managed to get it into preproduction. Cole had read it and been so impressed that he'd put Zach in contact with a few guys who might be interested in financing it. Within the month, Ed Saunders and Jim Granek had come up with enough money to finance some of the preproduction costs, giving Zach a better chance to pitch the project to a studio.

Though he didn't like giving away any control of the creative process, he had agreed to make Ed and Jim producers. He'd also brought in Alicia Warfield, another acquaintance from ATL, to act as assistant producer until the film went into production. The three of them were due to arrive at the offices in a half hour, shortly after he'd asked Kelly to come.

He and Kelly hadn't spoken since the day she'd left

Atlanta—though that hadn't kept him from thinking about her. Memories of their intimacies had stoked his fantasies nearly every night. He'd thought his feelings for her would have faded by now, but instead, they'd grown more intense.

Perhaps it was because he'd known all along they'd be seeing each other again. He wanted her for the lead role in his film—it had been written for her. And in order to do that, he'd have to see her again. There had never been any doubt in his mind about whom he'd cast and now the time had come to convince her that working with him wouldn't be a problem for either one of them.

She'd left a message on his cell phone yesterday, informing him that she'd be in Atlanta, and he'd taken some comfort in the fact that she wanted to see him again. But he'd decided not to call her back, to leave her hanging for a little while longer.

At least being with her again wouldn't be a problem on the surface. Zach wasn't sure how he'd feel once they were in the same room, alone. If all the old desires came back up, then he'd simply ignore them. It was obvious, after six weeks of silence, that she'd moved on with her life.

The phone on the credenza rang and Zach crossed the room and picked it up. "She's here," the receptionist said. "Do you want me to send her back?"

"Go ahead. And send the other three back as soon as they all arrive." Zach cleared his throat and smoothed his hands over the hips of his khaki trousers. He wore a blue oxford shirt and a tie, not his usual attire, but appropriate considering he wanted to look older than his twenty-four years.

Zach circled the table and waited near the door, wondering what it would be like when he finally saw her again. Would all the old desires suddenly come rushing back? Or would he be able to maintain an air of indifference? He found out an instant later when Kelly rounded the corner, her overnight bag slung over her shoulder. She walked past the conference-room door without even looking inside.

"In here," Zach called.

A few seconds later, she returned to the doorway, her beautiful face crinkled into a confused frown. "Zach?"

"Hello, Kelly. How are you?"

"What are you doing here?" She glanced around the room. "I'm supposed to meet with some people, producers and a director, about a…a film."

Zach took her bag and set it beside the credenza. "That would be me. Producer, director, writer."

"You? This is for your film?"

Zach nodded. "I got backing for my project. Our project, actually, since I'm going to give you cowriting credit for the film. We're starting preproduction now. And, if everything goes well, we'll film this summer."

"I thought you were going to wait until you got your lottery money."

Zach shrugged. "That could be tied up in court for months. So I decided to go out and find financing. I had some contacts, Cole Crawford had a few more, I called them up and they gave me enough to get started."

"That—that's wonderful," Kelly said, a warm smile breaking across her features.

Zach felt his pulse quicken and he fought the temptation to pull her into his arms and kiss her. "Yes, it is. And the first person that I thought to call was you. I want you to star in the film."

"Do you really?" Kelly asked.

"Of course I do. I wouldn't have asked you to come if I didn't. And the part was written for you. I can't imagine anyone else playing it."

A blush colored her cheeks and she glanced away. "When I first walked in, I thought maybe you wanted to see me for other reasons," Kelly said.

"No," Zach said.

"I see. You know, I called to let you know I was coming."

"I know."

"You didn't return my call."

"Because I knew I'd be seeing you. I didn't think there was a point." He pulled out a chair at the conference table and invited her to sit down. "Can I get you something to drink?"

Kelly shook her head. "Things have been going very well for me lately. I've had some interesting developments in my career."

"Your agent filled me in," Zach said, taking a place at the head of the table. "She sent me your resume. You must be very excited."

"I am. I finally feel I might have a career as an actress, and not just one where I'm scraping to make ends meet. I could buy a house. Not a big one, mind you. And maybe a new car."

"And that's what you want?"

"Well, it would make my life easier," she said.

"I'm afraid our film isn't going to pay that much."

"Oh, that doesn't make a difference," Kelly said. "I'm not that big that I can afford to turn down work. Especially interesting work."

"And you'll be all right working with me?"

"Of course. We're both adults, we can keep things on a professional level."

A knock sounded on the conference-room door and Zach quickly stood. He introduced Ed and Jim as his coproducers and Alicia as his assistant producer. Kelly shook hands with each of them before Zach nodded and they all sat down.

"Well, I wanted you all to meet Miss Castelle so you'd have an idea of where I was going with this story. I wrote the part of Dina with her in mind. Here's her resume and head shot." Zach withdrew a stack of papers from a file folder and handed them out to his colleagues. "Miss Castelle will be appearing in a new television series that's going to begin filming in a few weeks. It will air on the Fox network. By the time our film comes out, people will definitely recognize her name and her face."

"And since I'm not a big star yet, you can get me for cheap," Kelly joked.

Zach chuckled. "That's right. We'll be getting an actress who may just end up being a star by the time our film hits the theatres. Kelly, why don't you tell them a bit about yourself."

Zach listened as Kelly chatted about her career in Hollywood and her philosophies about acting. She was bright and personable and he could see that they were impressed. Zach explained how Kelly had provided much of the insight into the character of Dina through her own experiences as a struggling actress. And when she finished, Alicia looked at Jim and Ed and smiled.

"Well, you certainly would make a good Dina," she said. "But I have a few concerns. I just don't think we should make any firm casting commitments so soon. We won't go into production for at least six to eight months and if we hit a stumbling block, it could be years. I'm sure Miss Castelle doesn't want to tie herself down to a project for that long, especially if her future is as bright as you say it is."

"And we certainly shouldn't look at just one person," Jim continued. "This is a great script and there are going to be bigger actresses interested in playing this part."

"I wrote the role with Miss Castelle in mind," Zach said, trying to keep his irritation from coloring his tone. These people had promised to support his creative vision. And at the first available opportunity, they were questioning it! "She's the person I want."

Ed nodded. "I'm sure she is. But we're just asking you to take more time and consider all your options."

"If we don't book her now," Zach said, "she'll have other commitments. Bigger, more important films, I'll guarantee it. And then you'll all be sorry you didn't jump when you had the chance."

"Listen," Kelly said, interrupting their argument, "I don't

have to play this part. I want to. I'd love to play this part, but you're right, this film deserves to get made. And if I'm the stumbling block, then I'd be happy to step aside."

The trio stood up. "Well, it was a pleasure to meet you, Miss Castelle," Alicia said. "I can see why Zach is so keen to have you in his movie."

Kelly said goodbye to them all, then sat back down in her spot after they closed the door behind them. "Well, that wasn't so bad," she said with a smile. "They seem to be very anxious to make your film."

"Not so bad?" Zach shouted, shoving away from the table. "You gave away your part. Hell, Kelly, no wonder you didn't have any success in Hollywood: You can't just sell yourself short like that."

"I didn't. I told them I wanted the part."

He stood and began to pace the length of the conference room. "But you gave them an out. You let them think you'd be willing to walk away. I was here to fight for you and you let them leave here without a firm offer."

"I am willing to let it go. So that you can get your film made. That's the most important thing."

"My film will be made even if they don't back me. I won't have them dictating who I hire. I'll have my own money at some point. Hell, I'll have money coming out my ears between the lottery and the university lawsuit. But I don't want to do my film unless you do it with me."

"Come on, Zach, you know they're right. There probably will be a more famous actress interested in taking the role. The part is wonderful. And they won't care about the pay."

"They can't tell me who to cast in my project."

"You have to make compromises sometimes, just to get the work done."

"You can make compromises. But I don't have to. Not yet. This is my film and I'm going to make it the way I want it made. With you."

Kelly slowly stood, then moved into Zach's path. He stopped and held his breath. They were close enough to touch, close enough that he could feel the heat from her body and smell the scent of her perfume. Zach clenched his hands at his side to keep from reaching out and pulling her into his arms. All he could think about was the taste of her lips, the feel of her body beneath his hands.

He swallowed hard as he gaze met hers. "It's good to see you again," he murmured.

Kelly smiled. "You haven't changed a bit."

"You've gotten more beautiful," he commented.

"And you're just as charming."

Zach chuckled. "I'm sorry. I didn't mean to yell. We're all supposed to have dinner together tonight, so maybe I can convince them then. Hell, those two guys don't know anything about movies. They're real-estate investors. They build office parks and shopping malls."

"I planned to have dinner with Angie tonight," Kelly said. "But I can call and cancel. We can see each other tomorrow. Actually, I'm not flying out for a few more days. I changed the ticket you sent me."

"Good," Zach said. "Then that will give us more time...to work, I mean."

"Work," she murmured. "Right. So, I guess I'll go check into the hotel and you can let me know about dinner?"

"I'll take you over," he said. "It's not far. It would be silly to call a cab."

As they drove the short distance to Kelly's hotel, Zach tried to keep up a constant stream of polite conversation. He asked about her work and what she'd been doing in the weeks since he'd last seen her. And he tried not to refer to anything that had happened the last time she was in Atlanta. If she'd put their short but passionate affair in the past, then he wasn't going to be the idiot who brought it up in conversation. It would only prove one painful point—he hadn't gotten over her as quickly as she'd gotten over him.

He dropped her off in front of the hotel, helping her to the door with her overnight bag, then promised that he'd be back at six-thirty to pick her up for dinner. As he drove away, he congratulated himself on being able to make it through their first meeting without any major gaffes.

But that didn't erase the fact that he still felt an overwhelming desire for her. Just looking into her eyes made him ache, and the moments when they touched, however fleeting they might have been, made his pulse race and his body react. It had taken all his willpower just to remain calm and rational.

It would be easier at dinner. They wouldn't be alone, they'd be in a public place with three other people. If he could just make it through the evening, then he'd be fine.

She'd return to L.A. and he wouldn't have to think about her again until they began production on the film.

"Yeah, right," he muttered to himself. He hadn't stopped thinking about her from the moment they'd met two months before. And now that he'd seen her again, he didn't expect anything to change. He was still in love with her. But at least now, he knew where she stood.

"It was torture," Kelly cried as she sat down on the end of the bed. "From the moment I saw him, all I could think about was taking his clothes off and running my hands all over his naked body. And he looked like he barely even re-membered what we'd shared a few months ago."

Angie frowned as she distractedly rubbed her tummy. The moment she'd arrived at Kelly's hotel room, she'd crawled onto the bed, pulled a bag of saltines from her purse and listened as Kelly described the events of her meeting with Zach.

"Maybe he was pretending," she suggested.

"I don't think so," she said.

"Maybe he thinks that you don't care anymore so he pretends not to."

"You think?" Kelly asked. She shook her head, then picked up the sexy black dress that Angie had brought along. Kelly had packed clothes appropriate for a meet-ing, not a seduction. But by the time she'd returned to the hotel, Kelly had already decided that she and Zach would be sleeping in the same bed that night.

After all, what if this was the last opportunity they had

to be together? His investors might just convince him to hire another actress and then she'd never have an excuse to see him again. If this was it, then she planned to take full advantage of him.

"The only way you're really going to know is if you try to seduce him. If he goes along with it, then you have your answer," Angie said.

"And if he doesn't, I'll be horribly mortified and embarrassed and I'll never be able to face him again."

"Don't you think you're being a bit overdramatic?" Angie asked.

Kelly strode to the bathroom, the dress in hand. "I'm an actress. I'm allowed to be dramatic." She shrugged out of the robe, then pulled the dress up over her hips. She wasn't wearing any underwear, though Angie had brought along something new from the shop.

When she walked back out, Kelly twirled around. "What do you think? Sexy enough?"

"Yeah," Angie said. "Are you planning on going without underwear?"

"No bra," she said. "But I think I'll put on the panties, just so he has something to take off."

"Oh, and do the stockings, too," Angie suggested. "Men are just wild about those thigh-high stockings, especially with stiletto heels." She pointed to her belly. "That's how this baby was conceived, you know. Cole and I went out to a business dinner and I was wearing thigh-highs. He rubbed my leg under the table and after that, he couldn't keep his hands off me."

"Well, I can assure you we won't be making any babies tonight," Kelly said. "I bought a very large box of condoms this afternoon."

"Well, you're all set for fun then," Angie said, grinning. "Your hair looks fabulous, your makeup is perfect. Now, you just have to wait."

"He said he'd be here at six-thirty," Kelly said. "I've got fifteen minutes."

A knock sounded on the door and they looked at each other. "He's early," Angie said. She crawled off the bed, snatching her saltines and shoving them in her purse. "I think I'll be going now."

Kelly drew a deep breath and walked to the door, then pulled it open. Zach stood on the other side, a bouquet of flowers in his hand. He was dressed in a navy sport coat, khakis and a pale yellow shirt. "Hi," he said.

"Hi," Kelly answered, stepping aside to let him enter.

Zach chuckled when he saw Angie. "Hey, there," he said. "How are you?"

"Pregnant," Angie replied. "And getting bigger by the minute."

"You look wonderful," Zach said. He stepped up to her and gave her a hug, then glanced back at Kelly. "Are you glad to have her back in town?"

Angie nodded. "How about you?"

Kelly sent her a disapproving look but her friend just grinned.

"Yeah, it is nice to have her back," he said. Zach turned to look at Kelly, his gaze slowly drifting down her body and back up again. When he fixed on her face, Kelly felt her cheeks warm and her pulse quicken.

"Well, I'll leave you two to your...meeting," Angie said, walking to the door. "Zach, stop by the shop sometime. It's always nice to get a male perspective on the merchandise."

He chuckled, his gaze still fixed on Kelly's. "I'll do that."

The door clicked shut and Kelly smiled, suddenly aware that they were alone and she wasn't wearing any underwear. "I'd offer you a drink," she said, "but there's no minibar."

Zach held out the flowers and she saw that he was also carrying a bottle of champagne. "I brought something. I figured we might want to relax a bit before we left for dinner."

Kelly hurried to the bathroom to fetch two glasses. Zach set the flowers on the bed, then opened the champagne, the cork popping off and dropping to the floor. He poured a measure into each glass, then set the bottle on the bedside table.

"Should we have a toast?" Kelly asked.

He stared at her for a long moment, his gaze flitting over her features, as if he were searching for something. Then his eyes dropped to her lips. He seemed to be holding his breath, waiting for something.

"A toast?" she repeated.

"What?"

"To us," Kelly said. "And to your movie."

She held out her glass to Zach, but instead of knocking

it against his, he grabbed it and set it next to the champagne. In one easy motion, he wrapped his arm around her waist and pulled her against his body. Kelly gasped as his mouth came down on hers in a deep, penetrating kiss.

The shock of it all caught her completely off guard, but as he continued to tease at her lips with his tongue, she realized that she'd been waiting for this all along. This one moment, when the uneasiness between them simply dissolved and they were back to where they belonged—in each other's arms.

Zach murmured her name as his hands skimmed over her body, touching every curve before moving on. Then, he slipped beneath the hem of her dress, slowly sliding the fabric up along her thigh. When he realized that she wasn't wearing underwear, he froze and drew back.

"So you were expecting this?"

"I wanted this," Kelly said. "I've wanted this every day since I left Atlanta."

His eyebrow cocked up and he smiled, that devilish smile that had always sent shivers down her spine. "Naughty girl," he scolded.

"You're the one with your hands under my skirt," Kelly teased. "I wouldn't be calling names."

Zach laughed, then grabbed her waist again and pulled her toward the bed. "God, I've missed you," he murmured, and then kissed her. "I've missed your nose and your lips and your ears." He cupped her breasts in his hands. "I've missed your beautiful body and the way you smell. I even bought a bottle of your perfume so I could spray it on my pillow."

"You're crazy," Kelly said.

"Maybe I am. But it's a good crazy, isn't it?" He sat down on the edge of the bed and she stood between his legs as he gently ran his hands over her backside. "Do you know how long I've been waiting for you to call?"

"And I thought you didn't call because you we're over me. Over us," Kelly said.

"So we spent the last six weeks apart because we're both too stubborn to pick up the phone?"

"That, and I think we both needed time away, time to see how we really felt," Kelly said.

"And how do we feel?" Zach asked. "Would you like me to go first?"

Kelly nodded, running her hands through his hair. "Yes, please."

"I don't want be without you, Kelly Castelle. I don't care about all the things that you think are standing between us. I'm determined as hell to knock them down. I'm in love with you, Kelly. And I'm willing to do whatever it takes to make this work."

He grabbed her waist and pulled her down onto the bed, rolling her beneath him. His mouth found hers again and he kissed her, this time more gently, teasing at her lips with his tongue.

"And I'm in love with you, too," Kelly said, staring up at his handsome face.

He pulled the strap of her dress over her shoulder and bit her softly. Kelly arched against him and she could feel his shaft, hard and hot, through the fabric of his khakis. Her hands found his face and she smoothed her palms over his cheeks, staring at the man who'd stolen her heart and her soul.

"Make love to me, Zach."

"Now?"

She nodded. "I want to feel you inside of me again. I want it to be like it used to be between us."

"No," he murmured. "Not until you promise me that this is a beginning and not another end."

"It is," she said. "We belong together. I know that now."

"And we'll find a way to work this out?"

Kelly nodded.

"You know, it won't be easy. But I'm not going to give up," Zach said.

Kelly kissed him, gently and sweetly, her hands cupping her face. "Neither will I."

Zach grinned, then pulled her against him, nuzzling his face into her belly. "So what do you think we should do now? Now that we have our life planned out?"

"We probably should have some champagne and then go to dinner," Kelly said.

"I cancelled dinner," Zach said. "I was going to take you out and try my hardest to seduce you. But I guess you were more of a pushover than I thought you'd be."

Kelly gave him a gentle shove. "A pushover? You're calling me a pushover?"

"No. I just meant you were much easier than— Wait, that didn't come out right. You were more open to my point of view."

"I'll show you easy," Kelly said, scrambling to her

knees. She reached for the hem of her dress and slowly pulled it up, wriggling as she drew it over her head. When she opened her eyes again, she saw Zach staring at her, his eyes wide, a crooked smile on his face. "Now, that's easy."

She shoved him down on the bed and crawled on top of him, her legs straddling his hips. "I think you have far too many clothes on," she said.

"I think you're right," Zach replied. "Would you like to remedy that situation?"

They rolled around on the bed until Zach's clothes had all been tossed aside. And when he playfully pulled her beneath him and stretched out over her body, Kelly sighed softly. There were definitely benefits to falling in love with a younger man, she mused. But she no longer thought of Zach as younger. He was simply the man in her life, the man who loved her. The man who made her feel wonderfully and utterly complete.

Life just couldn't get any better, could it?

* * * * *

*Wait! We don't have any millionaires yet!
Don't miss Blaze #362
TALL, DARK AND FILTHY RICH by
Jill Monroe, the next book
in the* MILLION DOLLAR SECRET
miniseries, available next month.

Silhouette® Romantic Suspense
keeps getting hotter!
Turn the page for a sneak preview
of Wendy Rosnau's latest **SPY GAMES** *title*
SLEEPING WITH DANGER.

Available November 2007.

Silhouette® Romantic Suspense—
Sparked by Danger, Fueled by Passion!

Melita had been expecting a chaste quick kiss of the generic variety. But this kiss with Sully was the kind that sparked a dying flame to life. The kind of kiss you can't plan for. The kind of kiss memories are built on.

The memory of her murdered lover, Nemo, came to her then and she made a starved little noise in the back of her throat. She raised her arms and threaded her fingers through Sully's hair, pulled him closer. Felt his body settle, then melt into her.

In that instant her hunger for him grew, and his for her. She pressed herself to him with more urgency, and he responded in kind.

Melita came out of her kiss-induced memory of Nemo with a start. "Wait a minute." She pushed Sully away from her. "You bastard!"

She spit two nasty words at him in Greek, then wiped his kiss from her lips.

"I thought you deserved some solid proof that I'm still in one piece." He started for the door. "The clock's ticking, honey. Come on, let's get out of here."

"That's it? You sucker me into kissing you, and that's all you have to say?"

"I'm sorry. How's that?"

He didn't sound sorry in the least. "You're—"

"Getting out of this godforsaken prison cell. Stop whining and let's go."

"Not if I was being shot at sunrise. Go. You deserve whatever you get if you walk out that door."

He turned back. "Freedom is what I'm going to get."

"A second of freedom before the guards in the hall shoot you." She jammed her hands on her hips. "And to think I was worried about you."

"If you're staying behind, it's no skin off my ass."

"Wait! What about our deal?"

"You just said you're not coming. Make up your mind."

"Have you forgotten we need a boat?"

"How could I? You keep harping on it."

"I'm not going without a boat. And those guards out there aren't going to just let you walk out of here. You need me and we need a plan."

"I already have a plan. I'm getting out of here. That's the plan."

"I should have realized that you never intended to take me with you from the very beginning. You're a liar and a coward."

Of everything she had read, there was nothing in Sully Paxton's file that hinted he was a coward, but it was the one word that seemed to register in that one-track mind of his. The look he nailed her with a second later was pure venom.

He came at her so quickly she didn't have time to get out of his way. "You know I'm not a coward."

"Prove it. Give me until dawn. I need one more night to put everything in place before we leave the island."

"You're asking me to stay in this cell one more night…and trust you?"

"Yes."

He snorted. "Yesterday you knew they were planning to harm me, but instead of doing something about it you went to bed and never gave me a second thought. Suppose tonight you do the same. By tomorrow I might damn well be in my grave."

"Okay, I screwed up. I won't do it again." Melita sucked in a ragged breath. "I can't leave this minute. Dawn, Sully. Wait until dawn." When he looked as if he was about to say no, she pleaded, "Please wait for me."

"You're asking a lot. The door's open now. I would be a fool to hang around here and trust that you'll be back."

"What you can trust is that I want off this island as badly as you do, and you're my only hope."

"I must be crazy."

"Is that a yes?"

"Dammit!" He turned his back on her. Swore twice more.

"You won't be sorry."

He turned around. "I already am. How about we seal this new deal?"

He was staring at her lips. Suddenly Melita knew what he expected. "We already sealed it."

"One more. You enjoyed it. Admit it."

"I enjoyed it because I was kissing someone else."

He laughed. "That's a good one."

"It's true. It might have been your lips, but it wasn't you I was kissing."

"If that's your excuse for wanting to kiss me, then—"

"I was kissing Nemo."

"What's a nemo?"

Melita gave Sully a look that clearly told him that he was trespassing on sacred ground. She was about to enforce it with a warning when a voice in the hall jerked them both to attention.

She bolted away from the wall. "Get back in bed. Hurry. I'll be here before dawn."

She didn't reach the door before he snagged her arm, pulled her up against him and planted a kiss on her lips that took her completely by surprise.

When he released her, he said, "If you're confused about who just kissed you, the name's Sully. I'll be here waiting at dawn. Don't be late."

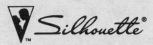

Romantic
SUSPENSE

Sparked by Danger,
Fueled by Passion.

Onyxx agent Sully Paxton's only chance of
survival lies in the hands of his enemy's daughter
Melita Krizova. He doesn't know he's a pawn in the
beautiful island girl's own plan for escape. Can
they survive their ruses and their fiery attraction?

Look for the next installment in the
Spy Games miniseries,

Sleeping with
Danger
by Wendy Rosnau

Available November 2007 wherever you buy books.

ATHENA FORCE
Heart-pounding romance and thrilling adventure.

History repeats itself...unless she can stop it.

Investigative reporter Winter Archer is thrown into writing
a biography of Athena Academy's founder. But someone
out there will stop at nothing—not even murder—to
ensure that long-buried secrets remain hidden.

ATHENA FORCE

Will the women of Athena unravel Arachne's powerful
web of blackmail and death...or succumb to their
enemies' deadly secrets?

Look for

VENDETTA
by *Meredith Fletcher*

*Available November
wherever you buy books.*

HARLEQUIN Romance.

New York Times bestselling author

DIANA PALMER

Handsome, eligible ranch owner Stuart York knew
Ivy Conley was too young for him, so he closed his heart
to her and sent her away—despite the fireworks between
them. Now, years later, Ivy is determined not to be
treated like a little girl anymore…but for some reason,
Stuart is always fighting her battles for her. And safe in
Stuart's arms makes Ivy feel like a woman…his woman.

Winter Roses

Available November.

REQUEST YOUR FREE BOOKS!

2 FREE NOVELS PLUS 2 FREE GIFTS!

HARLEQUIN®

Blaze

Red-hot reads!

HB07

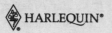

Cut from the soap opera that made her a star, America's
TV goddess Gloria Hart heads back to her childhood
home to regroup. But when a car crash maroons her in
small-town Mississippi, it's local housewife Jenny Miller
to the rescue. Soon these two very different women,
together with Gloria's sassy assistant, become fast friends,
realizing that they bring out a certain secret something
in each other that men find irresistible!

Look for

THE SECRET GODDESS CODE

by

PEGGY WEBB

Available November wherever you buy books.

HARLEQUIN®

N⅔xt™

TheNextNovel.com

HN88146